July 18th

Dear Doris,

Tonight I'm feeling like you are the only true friend I have and the only person I can talk to. I'm beginning to think that it was a mistake to come here. I should've just stayed in the group home. I try to fit in, but I don't, which doesn't make sense because the Smiths do everything they can to make me fit in. I try to be myself like I always used to be, but "myself" doesn't feel right anymore. I haven't felt like a part of things since I left you and all of my friends in the Bronx. . . .

Love,

Other books by Joyce Hansen
published by Clarion Books

The Gift-Giver
Home Boy
Yellow Bird and Me

ONE TRUE FRIEND

JOYCE HANSEN

CLARION BOOKS
New York

*To Dr. Henrietta M. Smith, for her friendship and
encouragement, and for her unwavering commitment
to the field of children's literature.*

*And to children everywhere who are searching for a
real childhood. May God bless you.*

Clarion Books
a Houghton Mifflin Company imprint
215 Park Avenue South, New York, NY 10003
Copyright © 2001 by Joyce Hansen
First Clarion paperback edition, 2005.

The text was set in 13-point Bembo.

www.houghtonmifflinbooks.com

Printed in the U.S.A.

The Library of Congress has catalogued the hardcover edition as follows:

Hansen, Joyce.
One true friend / by Joyce Hansen.
p. cm.
Summary: Fourteen-year-old orphan Amir, living in Syracuse, exchanges letters with his friend
Doris, still living in their old Bronx neighborhood, in which they share their lives and give each
other advice on friendship, family, foster care, and making decisions.
ISBN 0-395-84983-7
[1. Friendship—Fiction. 2. Choice—Fiction. 3. Letters—Fiction. 4. Orphans—Fiction. 5. Foster
home care—Fiction. 6. African Americans—Fiction 7. Bronx (New York, NY)—Fiction.] I. Title.
PZ7.H19825 On 2001   [Fic]—dc21   2001028483

CL ISBN-13: 978-0-395-84983-5   CL ISBN-10: 0-395-84983-7
PA ISBN-13: 978-0-618-60991-8   PA ISBN-10: 0-618-60991-1

VB 10 9 8 7 6

CONTENTS

Amir's Story

To Whom It May Concern:

I am looking for my aunt, Gloria Jones. I am also looking for my brothers and sisters. Their names are Olivia, Shawn, David, and Sharon. I think they all live in Manhattan, in New York City. We were separated about $2^{1}/2$ years ago when my parents died.

If you are Gloria Jones, or know where she is, please write to me at 324 Sylvan Lane, Syracuse, New York 13299. I have another brother, Ronald Daniels, who is seven years old, and we live together in Syracuse with Grace and Alvin Smith, our foster parents. My brother Ronald has been living with the Smiths since he was two years old. I've been here for the past three months. Before moving to Syracuse I lived in the Bronx, and before that I lived in Manhattan and Brooklyn.

Thank you very much for any help you can give me.

Sincerely yours,

Amir Daniels

Amir reread the letter very carefully. He wanted to add, *If you are Aunt Gloria, I'm sorry for what I did.* But he didn't. He'd apologize to her face if he ever saw here again in life. He read the letter once more and recalled one of his father's favorite sayings: *You got to make a good first impression if you want folks to pay attention.*

Amir made sure that every word was spelled correctly. He had another thought. In detective stories the cops always wanted to know the missing person's age. In his small, neat script that looked almost like printing, he included the ages that the children would be now: Olivia, 12. Sharon and Shawn (twins), 11. David, 9. I am 14 years old, he added.

Amir rewrote the letter and wondered whether he should add the Smiths' telephone number. No, better not—there'd be too many telephone calls, and some of them might be crank calls. The Smiths would be upset. *You gotta make things happen—can't just sit and wait for something to happen.* This time his father's deep voice ringing in his ears strengthened him, making him confident that his letter would end his long search. It would make something happen.

Amir planned to send the letter to the fifteen *G. Jones*es and two *Gloria Jones*es that he had found on the page torn from a Manhattan telephone book. He decided to draw pictures of himself and the children on another sheet of paper and include it with the letter. They would look a little different after all this time—but not that much. If his aunt saw his sketches, she'd know that his letter wasn't a fake.

Amir took his sketchpad and pencil case out of his backpack. He opened the drawer of the end table by the side of his twin bed and took out his pencil sharpener. While he sharpened his pencils to a fine point, he saw in his mind's eye the faces of his brothers and sisters as clearly as if they were standing before him; however, he decided to draw himself first, since he was the oldest.

He studied a recent snapshot of Ronald and him at the lake. He always thought it was kind of weird to draw yourself. Do people really know how they look? He quickly sketched his long, narrow face, high cheekbones, thin lips, and eyes so large and luminous that his friends in the Bronx used to call him Mr. Lightbulbs. He shaded in his face to suggest his rich brown complexion. Amir frowned at his self-portrait. One day he'd draw how he felt on the inside, if that was possible. He began to draw his sister Olivia next. His father used to say that Olivia had a "Grand Canyon smile, just like her mama's." He wondered whether Olivia still laughed a lot.

Amir didn't know how much time had passed and was beginning to draw the twins when the screen door slammed downstairs, startling him. "Hey, everybody, Big Papa's in the house," Alvin Smith boomed from the kitchen, as he always did when he came home from work.

Grace, Alvin's wife, giggled like a young girl and murmured a few words, but Amir couldn't hear what she said because her voice was so light and soft.

"I saw Ronald outside. Where's my other boy?" Alvin boomed loudly again.

Amir flinched as though he'd been pricked with a needle.

"Come on down here, Amir. I have something to tell you."

Amir put the letter and the sketches into his backpack and ran downstairs.

Alvin Smith's bulky six-foot frame seemed to take up all the space in the small kitchen. "I have some news," he said as he washed traces of dirt and cement off his hands.

Grace Smith sighed as she dried a mixing bowl. "Alvin, can't you wait for our family devotions?"

Alvin Smith wiped his hands and sat down heavily, motioning for Amir to sit opposite him at the kitchen table. The aroma of a freshly baked pound cake made Amir's mouth water as he forced himself not to get excited. Mr. Smith came home with good news every other day, but somehow it always turned out to be disappointing.

"I called my cousin Max, the social worker, today at lunchtime."

Amir nodded, his heart beginning to race despite his struggle to keep it still.

"Well, he told me your sisters and brothers had been living in separate foster homes at one time, but now they might be with your mother's sister in Queens. Seems like your aunt moved around a lot. He's checking that out for us. As far as he can tell, your brothers and sisters are with your aunt or other relatives in Queens. He's almost sure of it." Alvin Smith paused, taking out his handkerchief and wiping his wide dark brown face.

Amir tried not to feel anything. "But I don't have relatives in Queens. My aunt always lived in Manhattan." He thought of the fifteen names he'd found in the Manhattan telephone book and wondered whether he should tell Alvin Smith about the letter he'd just written.

The lines around Mr. Smith's mouth deepened. "Maybe they moved to Queens." He reached across the table and put his large hand on Amir's narrow shoulder. "Hey, don't look so sad, son. We've just about found them. It's only been three months that we been doing this serious search."

Amir's shoulders sagged slightly, but he quickly straightened them. *Buck up, you guys. Can't win the fight of life with your heads bowed. Won't see what's coming at you. Be determined.* His father's words again. Amir fastened his large eyes squarely on Mr. Smith. "But it's been over two years since I last seen them. That's a long time."

Grace Smith wiped her hands on her apron. "He's got a point, Alvin."

"But no one was seriously looking for them. Right, Amir?" Mr. Smith said.

"I was. I always asked everyone about them. The

counselors and caseworkers . . ." His voice drifted off as he wondered again whether he should tell Mr. Smith about the letter he'd written.

"What could you do, son? You're just a kid. Max is a social worker and knows how to search the records. You'd be surprised how papers—records and all—get mixed up."

"What about, uh, what about sending a letter to every Jones in Queens, then, or in Manhattan and the other boroughs?"

"You asked me about that once before, and I told you that I didn't think it was such a good idea." Mr. Smith fingered his mustache, which was sprinkled with gray. "I mean, that be like looking for a tiny splinter in a pig's butt." He reared back in his chair and laughed loudly at his own joke.

Mrs. Smith shook her head, but a slight smile appeared and vanished. "Alvin, please. Why can't you just say a needle in a haystack?"

"That's corny and ordinary."

"So is your joke," she said, as she carefully opened the oven door to check on the cake.

Amir didn't like the joke either, and for a moment he wondered whether Mr. Smith was making fun of him.

Be determined. "But Mr. Smith, I wrote a letter to send out."

Alvin Smith continued talking as though he

hadn't heard Amir. "My cousin is searching all kinds of records and addresses through his computer. That's the way you get information nowadays." He fingered his mustache again. "Anyway, we've already checked out every Jones we could find in the Bronx and Manhattan. Didn't miss a one—Ruth Jones, George Jones, Gregory Jones, June Jones, Mother Jones, and every other Jones in the book."

Amir lowered his eyes. He felt so stupid. His aunt was married, and perhaps her phone number and address were under her husband's name, Zachary. He'd have to look up Zachary Jones, too.

Mrs. Smith wiped her hands on her apron. "What did you say in this letter, Amir?"

His eyes brightened as he ran upstairs and quickly returned with the letter. He studied Grace and Alvin Smith as they read it together. Grace pursed her lips, and Alvin shook his head. "No, son. No. You'll have all kinds of nuts calling up here."

"But I didn't put in a telephone number."

"It doesn't matter, and like I told you before, this ain't gonna work."

Grace touched Amir's arm. Her glasses cast a silvery glow on her rounded cheekbones, and her voice was as smooth as her caramel-colored skin. "Amir, this is well written."

Mr. Smith handed the letter back to him. "My father would've torn this up in tiny pieces right in my face. I don't want to do you like that, 'cause I know this letter is about your life, and you put your heart into it, but I'm trusting *you* to tear it up."

Amir waited for Mrs. Smith to contradict her husband and tell him to save the letter and maybe send it out later. Instead she said, "My husband is right, Amir. This letter won't help, and it might attract some unwanted people."

She wiped her hands on her apron again. Amir knew that meant she was agitated or upset; her voice, though, always remained steady and soft, forcing you to listen in order to hear her. Amir liked her calm manner, but he couldn't understand why the letter worried her, too.

Mr. Smith put his arm around his wife. "Mama, you always have such a sweet way of expressing yourself. Amir, you'll attract some kind of psycho nut is what she doesn't want to say. Just have a little more patience. We'll find your aunt. You mentioned another aunt and uncle—the ones you ran away from that time. They live in Queens?"

"They weren't really my aunt and uncle, and they lived in Brooklyn. They took me in when we kids was separated."

"You sure, Amir?"

"I'm sure. They were some people my mother and father knew."

Mr. Smith removed the small notepad that he

always carried in his breast pocket. Sometimes he
Amir of a news reporter or a detective instead of a
bricklayer.

"Yes, that's right. I have their names here," Mr.
Smith said. He smiled encouragingly at Amir. "We'll
get through this red tape and bureaucracy mess, son.
We're just one step behind them. I want you to relax
and stay hopeful."

Mrs. Smith opened the oven again and removed
the cake. But Amir knew that she was listening, even
though her back was turned to them.

Mr. Smith stood up and walked over to the door.
"We'll find out where they are. You're sure there're
no other relatives—real or make-believe?"

"No, sir. Like I said, only my aunt, my mother's
sister. She used to visit us sometimes. . . ." His voice
trailed off, then he blurted out quickly, "I don't think
the letter will do any harm. It might help."

"Trust me on this one, son," Mr. Smith said. "I know
the devious things people do—especially to a kid.
Between me and Max, we'll find them. I'm sure of that."

Mrs. Smith turned away from the oven. "Don't say
sure, Alvin. The only thing we can be sure of is death
and taxes."

"But I can feel it, baby, deep, deep down in my
bones."

"That's your arthritis you feeling."

They both laughed, and even Amir smiled slightly.

Hesitating before he opened the door, Mr. Smith said, "You know what will help us solve this mystery of where your aunt is—if you can remember the last place you lived in when you and your whole family was together. I still don't understand why you can't remember that."

"Sometimes there are things people don't want to remember," Mrs. Smith said before Amir could answer. She walked over to her husband. "That's enough discussion for today." She turned to Amir. "We won't speak to you about this again until we have something definite to tell you. Isn't that right, Alvin?"

"Yeah, yeah, but I don't want him to lose hope." Mr. Smith opened the door. "Let me remind Ronald that we're having family devotions after I take my shower." He stopped and turned around again, as though he'd forgotten something. "Why don't you come on out here with your brother, son? School's over. Relax your mind for a while."

Children's laughter and the *bap bap bap* of a basketball drifted in from the front yard. "No, sir. Maybe later." He turned to Grace Smith. "Do you want me to help with the dishes tonight?" he asked.

"No, that's okay," She said. "It's Ronald's turn. Put on the television if you like. This is your home, too, you know."

Alvin Smith stood half in and half out of the doorway. "That's what I been telling him. And listen, you don't have to say 'sir.' Call me Pops. All of the younger guys on the job call me that."

Amir sighed and lowered his large eyes. "Yes," he mumbled.

Mrs. Smith gently pushed her husband out of the doorway. "You're letting in flies."

Amir hurried up the stairs, but he heard Alvin Smith trying to whisper, "What's wrong with him? Is he depressed? He's just too quiet."

He couldn't hear Grace Smith's response.

Amir sat on the edge of his bed and stared at the letter he'd written. Then he tucked it away in the end-table drawer under some old school papers. What difference would it make if he tore it up or just put it safely away? Mr. Smith had said the letter was about his life. How could he destroy his life?

Lately, the only way he could control the unhappiness that had begun to throb in a small corner of his brain was to either draw or write a letter to his best friend, Doris. Amir carefully tore a few sheets of paper out of his notebook. Whenever he wrote Doris, he was transported back to the Bronx, where, for a short time, he had been happy.

June 19th

Dear Doris,

How are you feeling? I hope you are happy. I'm writing you because I don't want to watch television or stand outside and look at my brother and his little friends play basketball. I'd rather "talk" to you.

What's happening on 163rd Street? Your last letter about graduation "madness" really made me laugh. I smile everytime I think of what you said about Yellow Bird's pants falling off his hips during graduation rehearsal. I hope Bird never forgets how you helped him with his school work. If it wasn't for you he might be repeating the sixth grade.

And what about Big Russell and T.T.? Are they still arguing over who's the best basketball player? And Mickey and Dotty, the twins? Have they calmed down? Or are they still acting immature, like you said. And Lavinia? Is she still being bossy? I guess everyone is excited about graduating from Dunbar and going to the seventh grade in September.

And how about those five sisters from Union Avenue, the ones you used to call the Nit Nowns because the baby sister said "nit nown" instead of sit down. Are you still friendly with them? Guess you're glad that summer vacation has almost begun.

Everything here in Syracuse is okay. This was the last day of school. I passed all of my subjects and will be going into the ninth grade. Thank you for the page from the telephone book. Hope nobody in your house needs it. I need another favor. See if there is a Z. Jones or Zachary Jones in the Manhattan book.

If there are only a few, could you send me the addresses and telephone numbers?

I wrote an "information wanted" letter today, and I was sketching pictures of my sisters and brothers to go along with it, but my foster parents don't want me to send it out. Mr. Smith likes to run everything his way. You know I don't want to make trouble or do things I'm not supposed to do, especially because the Smiths are so nice to me and are trying to help me. But I think that they are wrong about this letter. I feel I must send it out. What harm could it do?

I wish they didn't make such a big deal out of a little thing like a letter. I'm used to studying people. I wouldn't be tricked by some crazy child molester. What do you think, Doris? Should I send the letter anyway? One of my chores is to take the mail out of the box when I come home from school. I'll be working at a summer day camp starting next Monday, and so I'll still get the mail. Mrs. Smith has her own home cake-baking business. Usually she's so busy when the mailman comes, she never goes to the box. Anyway, the letters will be addressed to me, and the Smiths don't do things like open my mail. They would never know. Yet I feel guilty about sending it, because they trust me.

I've never lived with a foster family like them before, and sometimes I wonder when they'll change. They still treat me like I was their son. Mr. Smith tells me to call him Pops, but I can't say it. I never called any of the people I lived with anything except Mr. & Mrs. whatever their names were. Most times I just called them sir or ma'am. "Yes, sir" and "yes, ma'am" pleased them—especially the ones who were foster parents just for the money.

It's different for my brother Ronald. He calls the Smiths Mama and Papa, because he's lived with them since he was two. He's seven years old now, and they are adopting him, so he will be their son for real. He doesn't remember anything except living with the Smiths. If I was like him, then I wouldn't be so confused.

Mr. & Mrs. Smith always tell me that this is my home, too, but I still feel like a visitor. I hate it when Mr. Smith calls me "son." Then I get angry with myself for getting angry with him, because he is only being kind. I know that deep down he is a nice person. He calls all of Ronald's friends "son." I try to change my attitude, but my own father lives inside my head.

Lately Mr. Smith has started what he calls family devotions. He reads a passage from the Bible, and we talk about things that bother us and things that we are thankful for. It's a special family time, but it's hard for me to say anything except "Nothing's bothering me. I just want to find my brothers and sisters." The Smiths already know this. And then for the thankful part I say, "I thank God for the gift of life." My father always used to say that. I think Mr. Smith started this family devotions stuff as a way to force us to feel like a real family. I can't forget my mother and father just because I found a new family. When I stayed with people who didn't treat me like anything much, it was easier to pretend that my parents were still with me and that I was just visiting.

I'd make believe that my father was rolling up in his raggedy station wagon with my mother and the rest of the children, and we'd ride out to Coney Island. My mom would have sandwiches and potato salad, and if my father had extra money, we'd buy sodas and corn on the cob and my parents would eat raw clams on the half shell—ugh.

We'd stay on the beach all day; then in the evening we'd go on the rides. I know kids go to DisneyWorld nowadays, but Coney Island was our DisneyWorld. Thoughts about my mother and father make me feel happy and sad at the same time. I feel happy when I remember my father's rhymes and jokes, and then sad because I'll never hear his voice again—except in my imagination.

Still, Mr. & Mrs. Smith are the kindest foster parents I've ever had, and Syracuse, New York, is one of the nicest places I've ever lived in, but I still miss the Bronx even though I only lived there for five months. You and the rest of the 163rd Street crew are like my sisters and brothers. I don't think I ever told you this before, but even Mickey and Dotty remind me of my own twin brother and sister.

I didn't mean to write such a long letter. Just wanted to say hello.

Please write me back soon and give me all of the 163rd Street news—even the smallest event.

Love,

Amir

12 noon
Tuesday
June 23rd

My Dear Amir,

I was so happy to get your letter. Seems like we haven't "talked" for a long time. I've been saving up many things to tell you. My head is about to bust wide open, it's so stuffed with 163rd Street news.

The smallest event is that my baby brother, Gerald, is three years old now. I helped with his birthday party last Saturday. I had to teach ten little terror tots how to play musical chairs. Did you know that musical chairs turns kids into demons? But I kept those little crumb crushers in check. I did such a good job, my parents are trusting me to baby-sit Gerald all summer, and they're even paying me, so I guess you could say I have a summer job, too.

I still go to the Beauty Hive on Saturdays to help Miss Bee and the other hairdressers—mostly I answer the telephone and run errands. I love working there. My mother tells me to pay attention to what I'm doing and don't listen to all the gossip and grownup talk.

But my father calms her down—tells her that I know right from wrong and that they can't protect me from the world forever—which is the same thing I've been trying to tell my mother FOREVER!

Getting back to more important things:

I'm glad that the Smiths are nice to you. I don't think they will catch a bad attitude all of a sudden, do you? Three months is a long time. They would have changed by now. And just think, they took you out of the group home so that you and Ronald could live together, and they haven't stopped trying to help you, right? Just like you found Ronald, I bet you find the rest of your siblings. (New word I learned.)

It makes me feel real proud that you want my advice. Remember, you used to be the one who always gave me good advice. So here's what I think you should do about the letter. Send it out. Sometimes adults don't understand. Who're you hurting? No one. What could happen? Nothing, except you might find your aunt. Don't worry about the telephone book. My father brought it home from his job so we'd have a Manhattan phone book. No one uses it. We don't even know anyone in Manhattan.

I looked for Z. Jones and Zachary Jones, but didn't see that name.

After I read your letter, I thought about my own mother and father, and I was able to put myself in your sneakers and understand how you feel. I would feel the same way you do if I had to live with strangers—even nice ones. It would be like forcing my foot into a shoe that didn't fit. I know it would hurt.

As much as my parents' stories about growing up and their "how to behave in public" lectures get on my nerves, I could never think of anyone but them as my mom and dad. It would be hard for me to put a smile on my face and feel happy living with strangers. I might even be rude, and I know you could never be rude, Amir. When I'm sad, I get mad and evil as a snake and take it out on everybody, which I know is wrong. But like my father always says, "I'll work on that." I'm sure you're still acting sweet and kind even though you're unhappy. I bet you're too shy to speak at Mr. Smith's family devotions. It's hard enough to tell your real parents what you really feel.

Family devotions is an interesting idea, though. But if my family had such a thing, Gerald would be running around not paying attention. If I said something was bothering me, then my parents would tell some story to show me how lucky I am. So the what's-bothering-me part and the something-to-be-thankful-for part would be mushed together, and I'd end up thinking I'm supposed to be thankful for what's bothering me.

Then my mother would find the longest part of the Bible to read, and we'd all fall asleep and accidentally bang our heads on the floor before she said amen. Then we'd end up going to the emergency room. Maybe I'm exaggerating, but I'm sure something weird would happen.

I thought a lot about what you said about being happy and sad at the same time. Everything has two sides to it—a front and a back, a happy and a sad, a good and a bad. You get my drift? I can have a pity party one minute and a celebration the next. Some people, though, say that's a girl thing.

Think upon this. Imagine that your mother and father are in heaven watching out for you like guardian angels.

This is what I believe: When parents die while we're still kids and really need them, even though they don't always understand us, they become our guardian angels and look out for us from above. That's a positive thought for you today.

But I have one question. The raggedy station wagon you mentioned. Was that the car your parents had the terrible accident in?

I never told you this before because I didn't want you to be angry with me—like I was putting your business in the street—but we had to write an essay about someone who was determined to succeed. I wrote about you. I didn't use your name, and I kind of changed things around so no one would know it was you.

I wrote about a little boy (I made him six years old so he could really be small and weak—the teacher thought that was the most ridiculous part of the story). Anyway, just like you, this kid is determined to find his missing brothers and sisters; therefore, he bugs every social worker, counselor, caseworker, and teacher he meets until people get so tired of him bothering them, they help him. You told me that you used to bug every counselor you met about your missing family.

The point of the story was that the kid never gave up. I got a lousy grade on it. The teacher told me that I was supposed to write about a real hero or heroine. But I think what you did was great. You succeeded because you *made* someone help you. That's heroic. Do you know how hard it is to get good grownup help these days? You never did tell me how you actually ended up living with the Smiths.

I just thought of something. Our graduation speaker, who was a little boring, said one interesting thing—well, maybe more than one, but I wasn't paying strict attention. He said, "We will get back in life what we send out." I have thought a lot about what that means. If you're evil, then evil things will

happen to you. If you're kind, like you are, then
good things will happen to you. I think it's time for
the world to treat you kind, because you do not have
an evil bone in your body.

Now, here is the Big Event: All of the 163rd
Street/Union Avenue crew graduated yesterday.
Mickey and Dotty, the unidentical twins, are still
sawed off. They haven't grown an inch in their bodies
or their minds. Lavinia is still bossy and showing off.
She wore the biggest and whitest dress, like it was
her wedding day instead of sixth-grade graduation.
Big Russell is so wide now, he looks like a man.
Yellow Bird won the talent award, and I won the
English award and a perfect-attendance award, too;
however, my parents should get the perfect-
attendance award. If I was too sick to move, they'd
drag my sick body to school so I'd be marked present.

The big graduation surprise was Charlene. You
remember her—she's one of the five sisters from
Union Avenue you asked about, the Nit Nowns.
She's the quiet one. Well, Charlene received the
outstanding-student award. Her mother and her
sisters were there, and you know how loud those
sisters are, especially the older ones. When Charlene
walked up on the stage, the sisters stood up and
cheered like they were at a football game. Their
mother, Miss Connie, pulled them back in their seats.
Charlene looked so ashamed when everyone started

laughing at her family. I felt sorry for her and tried to put a muzzle on the twins, who thought it was so funny. "Why don't you be quiet?" I said. "She's embarrassed." The twins kept laughing anyway.

T.T. was the only one who didn't graduate. I knew he'd never get out of the sixth grade. He's supposed to be going to summer school, but he must be majoring in basketball. Seems like he's either on 163rd Street or in the playground day and night playing ball.

Graduation was fun, though, and now everyone is getting ready for the next grand event—the annual 163rd Street July 4th Block Party. The block party is big-time now, not the dinky little chip-and-dip affair that it used to be when you lived here. We're having a double-dutch contest, and whoever wins will take part in a citywide double-dutch tournament. We put together a double-dutch team with Charlene and her sisters. So now we have one team: The 163rd Street/Union Avenue Double Dutch Champs.

The 163rd Street crew told me to tell you hello. Inquiring minds want to know when you are coming back to the Bronx to visit us. Maybe this summer? How is your job at the day camp? Do you have a lot of terror tots to take care of?

I'm keeping my fingers, toes, and eyes crossed for you, and hope that you get together with all of your family soon. I have to go. Gerald is whining for me to fix him lunch, and my mother will be calling on the phone any minute now to check on us.

                              Love,

                              Doris

P.S. Try this: Practice saying Pop Smith and Mom Smith in letters to me. Maybe one day you'll be able to say it to them.

                                        June 26th

Dear Doris,

How are you? I was so happy to get your letter. I read it again this morning before I left for my job at the day camp. It made me feel like I was back in the Bronx. I feel sorry for T.T. Maybe one day he'll grow up. I am the counselor for the six- and seven-year-olds, and while they're napping, I'm writing to you.

I like this job very much. It reminds me of how I took care of my younger sisters and brothers. The other counselor teaches them how to swim and play games, and I do the arts and crafts. I'm going to show them how to make puppets this afternoon. Mostly, the children like to see me draw, and they always ask me to draw pictures of them.

Mr. Smith promised when I first moved in that

one day he'd drive me down to the Bronx for a visit, but he works most weekends, especially in the summer. It's a five-hour drive. One day, though, I'll visit you and the rest of the crew.

I never thought about guardian angels and stuff like that, but maybe you're right. Maybe my parents are still watching out for all of us—including Ronald. It's a positive thought, anyway, and it makes me feel good. Yes, the station wagon was the car that my parents had the accident in. They died in that car.

You're smart—that's why I asked your advice. I haven't sent out any letters yet, but I decided I will, even though I feel a little guilty. I have to send them. But like you said, who am I hurting? There's a Xerox machine here at the camp. When I asked the woman who works in the office whether I could make a copy, she said no one is allowed to use the machine but her, and she'd make me a copy when she had time. Then she started asking me a lot of nosy questions, like what is it for? Is it personal or official business? Is it something for my mother or father? I'm afraid she'd read the letter and tell the whole camp everything in it.

Sometimes there's a teenager working there. I'll ask him to let me make a copy when the woman isn't around.

When you said that you get back in life what you send out, you reminded me of something I had forgotten—my dad used to say the same thing in his own funny way. "Send out junk, and junk will fly back in your face." He also used to say, "When you help somebody else, you help yourself, too."

It makes me sad to remember. I guess I push some memories down deep inside myself until they disappear. Still, they return, sharp like needles. You're right about the Smiths, though. Why would they change now? They were nice to me from the first time we met. Sorry you didn't get an A for your story. The next time you need to find a famous person, try the encyclopedia. I ain't no hero.

There's not much to the real story of how I found out where Ronald was living.

I bugged the counselors, like I told you before. I'd always ask about my brothers and sisters. Most times caseworkers and counselors would try to help me. No one ever said no to me. They'd say, "We'll find out," but they never did. Either they never had the time or they forgot. My father always told me to be a pest when it's necessary. He'd say, "Sometimes a little ant in your pants can get your attention quicker than a rhino at your heels."

So I'd try to be a pest as much as I could, but you know me, Doris, I'm not too good at pestering. If I was, I'd figure out a way to pester that woman in the office into making copies for me. Anyhow, I talked to a counselor in the Bronx who found out that Ronald lived in Syracuse with the Smiths. At first

I thought that all of my brothers and sisters lived up here. It was because of her that I was sent to the group home up here, so I could be near him.

I never saw or heard from her again after that. She was a real nice lady, though. She contacted the Smiths, and they brought Ronald to visit me in the group home.

It was a sad visit. I didn't recognize Ronald, and he didn't know me. The last time I'd seen him, he was just a little kid. He stared at me with a big question mark in his eyes when Mrs. Smith said, "Ronald, meet your brother Amir."

Ronald knows that he's being adopted, and he knows that he has brothers and sisters, but I don't think he understands, even though the Smiths explained it to him. It's just something he was told. Ronald was calling the Smiths Mama and Papa, and it was hard for me to think of him as my brother.

I don't want to feel like that, because he is my brother. I kept reminding myself of how it was when my mother brought him home from the hospital. He had tiny hands and feet as soft as velvet. I remember how the rest of the kids always wanted to hold him and play with him, and my mother and father had to shoo them away. "Y'all going to kill this baby with love," my mother would joke. "You'll drown him with those slurpy kisses."

I was the only one who could hold him all of the time, because I was the oldest. He has no way of remembering how much we loved him. "You can call and visit your brother anytime," the Smiths told me. When you're a foster kid like me, you have to learn people fast. I could feel deep down inside my heart that they meant what they said. I know you're not supposed to judge a book by its cover, but they didn't seem like evil people—they looked like nice grandparents you could trust. Ronald stuck near them, like he was afraid of me.

Every week after the first visit, the Smiths picked me up and took me to church and then to their house for Sunday dinner. Mrs. Smith is a good cook and baker. She makes the best fried chicken in the world. Maybe the Smiths were the ants in my pants. They kept telling me that I could stay with them. "Ronald started out as our foster child," Mr. Smith would always remind me, "and now he's going to be our son for real." He also told me that he'd help me get in touch with the rest of my family.

I thought about it for a long time, because, like I said before, I felt deep down inside myself that the Smiths were real nice, honest people, but I was afraid that there could be another side to them. Also, Ronald acted like we wasn't even related. He still acts that way most of the time. Doris, I can tell only you this—it doesn't feel like he's my brother. But I guess he is, unless he's the wrong Ronald. (Just joking.)

After one of their visits Mr. Smith said, "My cousin is doing a search for your family's records. Me and Mrs. Smith want to help you, whether you live with us or not." That convinced me to stay with them. They wanted to help me just because that's the way they are.

They had a welcome party for me when I moved in. Mrs. Smith baked a huge chocolate cake, and some of the people from their church and the neighbors came. It was real nice of them, but I felt strange. I was used to being a foster kid and going to live in other people's homes, but I guess I wasn't used to getting a welcome party.

So there's some more of the story for you to tell—but I still think you'd better find a hero in the encyclopedia. (Smile.) It was just good luck that the Bronx counselor found out where Ronald was. I didn't really do anything so special.

By the way, writing Mom and Pop Smith is not going to make it any easier for me to say it. Anyhow, I don't suppose I'll ever have to. Once I get in touch with my aunt, I guess I'll be living with her. Well, I see some little eyes staring at me. The terror tots are waking up. Write back soon.

Love,

Amir

8:30 P.M.
Saturday
July 4th

My Dear Amir,

I hope that you are very, very fine and that your 4th of July was better than mine, and I hope that Mr. Smith is able to bring you down here soon. It's a real drag when you can't be with your best friend. Before I tell you about my stupid 4th of July, I want to say that I always imagine how you feel—to have parents who are not really your own parents. You see, I can't be a helpful friend if I can't understand exactly how you feel and try to feel the same way.

Like I said before, guardian angels led you to the Smiths. That's why they're nice to you. They can't help themselves. You probably shouldn't worry about not being able to call the Smiths Mom and Pop. When those same guardian angels lead you to your family, you won't be living with the Smiths anymore anyhow. However, I have a question. Why did you say in your last letter that you *guess* you'll be living with your aunt? Isn't that what you want more than anything else?

Let's put this good thought out in the world so that it can come back at you: Your brothers and sisters live in Manhattan or the Bronx with your aunt, you and Ronald will move back here to be with them, and everyone will live happily ever after. Except the Smiths, because I think they really like you and they'll miss you, and they love Ronald, so they'll miss him even more. But they'll come and visit you and Ronald every Sunday.

That's a nice fairy tale, ain't it, Amir? It would be so wonderful if things turned out that way, wouldn't it? Guess I'm bugging. No matter how things turn out, someone is going to be unhappy.

Here's another nice fairy tale: You move back to the Bronx. Then I wouldn't have to be bothered with my phony little girlfriends who can't be trusted.

Without you, Amir, I wouldn't have a sensible person in this world to talk to. I can't even talk to my parents anymore. No matter what happens in life, they make endless speeches about their own childhoods, which have nothing to do with my problems. My father tells me about his boyhood down South, and my mother tells me about her girlhood in Harlem, and I can't get a word in edgewise.

Guess you're wondering what in the world I'm ranting about, and what I'm doing in the house so early—the one night of the year when my parents let me sit out on the stoop until way after the sreetlights come on.

Remember I told you in my last letter that we were having a big 4th of July block party and double-dutch contest? And that now we had a 163rd Street/Union Avenue double-dutch team with Charlene and her sisters from Union Avenue?

Well, Lavinia and Mickey and Dotty decided that they did not want to be on a team with the sisters anymore, and that we should have two separate teams. Me, the twins, and Lavinia would be one team, and Charlene and her sisters another team.

Lavinia and the twins got angry with me. They said I was a traitor because I wouldn't go along with their scheme. They thought if we won the tournament in the fall, we'd travel all over the country and be on television. They think they're too cute to be on the same team with Charlene and her sisters, and are always talking about how funny the sisters look with those extensions in their hair, and how Charlene's clothes are always too big for her and how tall and skinny the older sisters are. If the truth be told, the only way Lavinia and the twins could have had a winning team was to keep those sisters on it. Those sisters are like double-dutch geniuses.

I like the sisters—even if we're not serious hang-out buddies. They've always been nice to me; they're just loud, except for Charlene. So I threatened to leave the team if Lavinia and the others threw the sisters off.

"I'm not a phony," I told Lavinia. "Just because you think this tournament is some kind of big deal, now you too good to associate with Charlene and her sisters after they taught you everything you know." You know what Lavinia had the nerve to tell me? "See ya," she said, flicking her hand at me like I was a nobody and a nuisance. "If you feel that way, go and hang out with them drugged-up sisters."

Now, how vicious is that? The sisters act wild, but I know they don't mess with drugs. Lavinia thinks they do because the sisters are always jumping double dutch in the playground, which is filled with teenagers, and that must mean they're up to no good. And Mickey and Dotty think whatever Lavinia wants them to think.

The playground may be a little worse than when you lived here, Amir. Yellow Bird, Big Russell, and the rest of the boys play basketball on the block and don't even go there anymore. Only T.T. still plays there. He and Charlene and her sisters all live in the same building across the street from the playground, so that's where they play.

People say that kids from the next block are fooling with drugs, but you know how everyone in this neighborhood exaggerates. Before the summer is over, there'll be more rumors than flies on 163rd Street. I'm glad I'm out of all of it and don't have any friends except you. I'm better off just staying by myself.

You see, Charlene's sisters got angry with me, too, because they think I didn't want them on the team either. I tried to explain to them that breaking up the team wasn't my idea. I even offered to stay on their team. They laughed in my face. "When you learn how to jump," one of them said. Only Charlene listened to what I had to say. "Don't pay them any mind," she said when they started yelling at me. "I believe you." Looks like no matter how nice I try to be, I make somebody mad.

So since I'm no longer on the stupid double-dutch team, I just sat on the stoop on the 4th of July and watched everyone else have a good time.

I know I'm not a good jumper—my long legs get in my way—but my ex-friends replaced me with a girl who doesn't even know how to turn the ropes good, much less jump. The poor child has no rhythm. The sisters won first place in the contest, and Lavinia and the twins won absolutely nothing. So you see, if Lavinia and Mickey and Dotty had listened to me and kept a single team, then we all would've been winners.

Anyway, all I need is one true friend who I can trust with my very life. You.

To be fair, there were also a few laughs today. Someone exploded a firecracker that made Miss Nichols's wig pop off her head like the lid on a steaming pot. I'm sure your 4th of July was much more sensible.

Bye for now. Oh, I almost forgot to ask—did that Old Battle-Ax in the office let you make some copies of your letter and drawing yet? If not, send them to me. My mother works in a cleaners', and they have a copying machine.

Your friend to the end,

Doris

July 9th

Dear Doris,

How are you doing? Thank you for offering to make copies of the letters for me, but the woman in the office was out today. (She's not that old. She's a Young Battle-Ax.) Her helper let me make all the copies I wanted. I copied five letters and five sketches. I didn't want to overdo it, otherwise he might not let me come back later to make more.

Yesterday Mr. Smith told me that he'd found out for sure that my sisters and brothers are with my aunt and her husband. All they have to do now is find her. I'm afraid to get excited, because I'll be disappointed if it's some kind of mistake. I said I *guess* I'll be living with my aunt because like Mrs. Smith always says, nothing is sure. Maybe my aunt won't want me to live with her. Maybe there's too many of us for her to take care of. Anyhow, at least the children are all together, and I will know where they are. When I finish high school and get a job, then they can all live with me. That's my plan.

Mr. Smith is still asking me to try and remember the last place we lived because that was the last time my aunt visited us. But all of my memories are useless. I can't remember exactly where we lived. I see a lot of different places in my head, and I don't know whether I'm remembering two different places like they were one. I think about a place we lived in the city, and I see a narrow street and that steep hill on Third Avenue and my mother walking out of a courtyard. I mix up 163rd Street in the Bronx with another place that I'm not sure of.

My 4th of July wasn't as exciting as yours. Most of the kids around here are seven- and eight-year-olds, like Ronald. Maybe I'll make friends when I go to high school. Except if friends visit me, they'll wonder why I call my parents Mr. and Mrs. Smith. (Ha, ha.) Mr. Smith drove us to the lake on the 4th. We had a picnic and saw a fireworks show in the evening. I missed the Bronx, though—sitting on the stoop, watching wigs pop off heads. Real fun.

Ronald had a good time playing basketball. He really thinks that he's going to grow up to be a famous basketball player. Ronald reminds me of Yellow Bird and Big Russell and the rest of the 163rd Street crew. Basketball is everything! Maybe that's why he's not so close to me the way you think a little brother would be. Guess he thinks I'm weird, since I don't play basketball and can't teach him anything about it.

When I first moved here, I tried to tell him about our family and tried to teach him how to draw, but he doesn't care about that. He tunes me out whenever I try to tell him anything. His eyes look blank, and he says, "Yeah, yeah, whatever." He acts like he wants me to hurry and shut up. I try hard not to be angry with him and to understand him. He was so young when we were together before. I wonder what the other kids are like now. I wonder if they remember me and our parents.

About Lavinia and the twins.

They're just being themselves. I think that they changed because the double-dutch contest became a big event. And maybe they look down on the sisters because they don't always have new clothes and they're sort of poor.

People used to do that to my family. My mother would say, "They don't know us, so they don't know what they're missing." I guess people talked about us because we were different. But I didn't know that we were different. I thought that all families were like us.

We used to put on family plays just for ourselves. My father played the piano, and when he wasn't away on the road, he'd play music for us. My mother made the costumes, and we kids made up a story with songs. Actually, I'd sketch pictures and the kids would put words to my drawings and turn it into a story. I can draw a story, but not tell one. My sister Olivia loved to sing.

I just thought about something, Doris. Maybe the plays were like our special family devotions. They were different from the Smiths', but they made us feel happy, even though we didn't pray and read the Bible.

You said that your parents like to talk about their childhoods. My mother always talked about growing up in the South, too, like your father does. She loved plants and flowers, so everywhere we lived looked like the Bronx Botanical Garden. She'd find half-dead plants because they were cheap. We'd help her clean and water them and watch them grow and flower. She'd tell us that we were like her geraniums—she wanted to help us grow and flower, too.

In some places she had the fire escape filled with plants. She loved red geraniums best of all. She used to say, "It's not where you live, but how you live."

Doris, it's time to eat dinner, so I'm going to go now. Write soon. Don't let Lavinia and the twins worry you. You'll figure out a way to make up.

Love,

Amir

P.S. Ignore the drug rumors.

12 noon
Tuesday
July 14th

My Dear Amir,

I was so happy to get your letter. Before it came, I was bored to tears. The only interesting time in my life is on Saturdays, when I work at the Beauty Hive, and on any day that I get a letter from you. I have a Suggestion for Today: *Think Only Positive Thoughts: My Letter Will Find My Aunt. My Aunt Will Find My Letter. I Will Live with My Aunt and My Sisters and Brothers Happily Ever After.*

You're not thinking straight—you're bugging. Why do you say your memories are useless, Amir? There's no such thing as a useless memory. Maybe you just don't want to remember things because they make you sad. Anyway, I'm glad you finally made copies of your letter and sketch. I don't know why grown people always want to be in our business. It's not like you're doing anything wrong—just trying to get some information.

Your family was different, especially from the Smiths, but I think that was a great thing—putting on family plays. Maybe that really was your family's way of having devotions. That could never happen here, unless we played church. My mother and father would preach, and me and Gerald would be the congregation—nodding and saying amen.

I don't have much news, because I lead a very dull life. Here is my typical boring day:

9:30 A.M.

Take Gerald to the library for storytime and pick out a book for myself. Yesterday and today I ran into Charlene in the library. She brought along her baby sister, Claudette. Charlene and I picked out books together. She likes to read, too.

10–10:30 A.M.

Walk home real slow so that Gerald will think we've been outside for a long time.

10:30–12 NOON

Let Gerald overdose on kiddie shows while I read, and then we eat lunch. My mother calls up on the telephone to make sure everything is okay.

12:30–1:30 or 2 P.M.

If I'm lucky, Gerald takes a nap and I either read or look out the window. There's always something interesting to see on 163rd Street, even when it's too hot to be outside—kids playing in the fire hydrant; Yellow Bird and them playing serious basketball with a bottomless milk crate tied to the lowest rung on the fire escape of my building (that milk crate is the tackiest thing you ever saw); Lavinia and the twins walking up and down and back and forth trying to look cute, or jumping double dutch.

2-3 P.M.

Gerald wakes up and whines about going outside. So I
read to him, and that keeps him quiet for 15 minutes.
Then we sit on the fire escape, but he's learning that
sitting on the fire escape is not the same thing as going
outside to play.

3:30 P.M.

My mother comes home from work and tells me that I
can go and play until suppertime. I go, because if I don't,
she'll start questioning me about why don't I want to go
outside, did I argue with my friends? Then she'll say that
I'm moody and that's why I don't have any friends.
When I go outside, Lavinia and the other girls are there
either sitting on the stoop gossiping or jumping double
dutch. They're still going to be in the tournament in the
fall. (Yellow Bird told me.) They don't say anything to me,
and I don't say anything to them. We make one another
invisible. I walk around the corner like I really have
somewhere to go. Me and Bird are still okay with each
other. He said that he was going to write you a letter.
However, I'd advise you not to hold your breath waiting.

4:00 P.M.

I go back upstairs and help with dinner. My mom's so
tired that she doesn't ask me why I came upstairs so soon.
She needs my help. I know she suspects that I've fallen
out with my friends. Any day now I'll get a lecture.

6:00 P.M.

My father comes home from work and we eat.

That's the story of my interesting life. I don't even keep a diary, because I'd be writing the exact same thing every day. I wouldn't even have to write anything. Just put in a new date and write "Ditto"— except for Saturdays at Miss Bee's.

I've thought of another thing I can do for you since I have so much time on my hands. I can look up florists and find out who sells red geraniums. Then I'll ask whether a woman with children used to come into the store to buy geraniums. What do you think of that idea?

Also, why did your parents move so much? Were you guys moving when your parents had the car accident? Was Ronald an infant when all of this happened? I don't mean to be nosy—just wondering. Guess I need to get a life. Bye for now.

Friends 4
v
e
r
Doris

P.S. Amir, please draw me a picture of the lake where you spent July 4th. Put Ronald in the picture, too. I want to see whether he looks like you. I miss your stupendous drawings.

part two

Brothers

Amir put the letter from Doris into his backpack. He took out his sketchpad, sat down on the bed, and recalled the deep blue-gray water of the lake and the fat white clouds floating like sailboats across the sky. He promised himself that he'd buy paints or colored pencils when he got his first paycheck.

He re-created the fluffy clouds that seemed as though you could curl up inside them. As his pencil moved quickly over the page, another image formed in his mind, and he began to draw a woman with a wide smile and deep dimples on either side of her chin. He heard his father's voice. *Darlin', you just smiling to show off them dimples.* Amir sketched in another face inside the swirl of clouds—a young man, with a narrow face and large, full eyes.

Suddenly Ronald burst into the room. "Amir, Mama says it's time to eat."

"Wait a minute. Look at this."

Ronald's eyes darted to Amir's sketch.

"Who's those people?" he asked, practically leaping on the bed.

Amir hesitated. "Our mother and father."

Ronald frowned. "That don't look like them."

"It's *our* mother and father," Amir said.

"It don't look nothing like them. I don't think you draw so good."

"I mean *our*—yours and mine."

Ronald stared at Amir blankly; then, before Amir

could stop him, he snatched the drawing out of Amir's hand and dashed out of the room.

"Wait, Ronald," Amir called, running down the stairs behind him.

Amir heard him shouting, "Mama, Papa, look what Amir did. He drew a picture of you, but it don't look nothing like you."

When Amir reached the kitchen, Ronald was waving the drawing like a banner. Alvin and Grace Smith both looked confused. Then Mr. Smith grinned as he took the drawing from Ronald. "Oh, man, this is great, son." He held the sketch at arm's length. "Look at this, Mama. The boy's got talent. Look at how he captured your beauty, Peaches."

Mrs. Smith giggled. "You go on with your foolishness." She looked over her husband's shoulders. "This is beautiful, Amir. You have a gift." She shook her head in disbelief. "You're so young to be able to draw like this."

"But it don't look like you," Ronald insisted.

Mrs. Smith's eyes clouded behind her glasses as she glanced at Amir and then turned away. "Artists can draw people to appear any way they want to, Ronald."

Amir said nothing, but his face burned with anger.

Mr. Smith, still holding the drawing at arm's length, smiled. "I like it. It looks just like me. What I like about it most is how young Amir made me look. So can I keep it now? I want to show those young scamps at work how good my son made me look."

Amir averted his eyes. "I'm not finished with it yet, sir . . . I mean Mr. Smith . . . I mean . . ."

"Amir, I told you about that sir business. I don't know why you—"

"Come on, food's getting cold," Mrs. Smith interrupted gently. "Let the boy finish his drawing." She took it out of her husband's hand and gave it back to Amir.

After supper was over and he'd helped clean the kitchen, Amir went outside to the backyard, where Ronald and Mr. Smith were playing one-on-one basketball.

Mrs. Smith stepped outside, too. "Alvin, you have no business stepping so high around this yard with Ronald," she said. "You won't be able to move a muscle tomorrow morning."

"I'm beating this kid, Grace," he said, huffing and puffing. "You know I was a star in high school."

"You'll be a fallen star, trying to keep up with a seven-year-old."

Ronald laughed. "Hey, Papa, look at this move." He dribbled around Mr. Smith's legs and threw the ball so that it hit the backboard and spun around the rim of the basket before falling inside.

"Look at this kid!" Alvin shouted.

Ronald, grinning proudly, threw the ball at Mr. Smith. "Come on, Papa, let me beat you again."

Amir went inside the house and ran upstairs. He took Doris's letter out of his backpack and reread it before answering.

July 18th

Dear Doris,

Tonight I'm feeling like you. You are the only true friend I have, and the only person I can talk to. I'm beginning to think that it was a mistake to come here. I should've just stayed in the group home. I try to fit in, but I don't, which doesn't make sense because the Smiths do everything to make me fit in. I try to be myself like I always used to be, but "myself" doesn't feel right anymore. I haven't felt like a part of things since I left you and all of my friends in the Bronx. Also, Ronald is not the way I thought he'd be. He acts more like Mr. Smith. Neither one listens when you try to explain things to them. They're both excitable.

Ronald did something this evening that made me so angry, I had to keep reminding myself about how he once was a little baby we loved so much. If I didn't think about that time, then I'd almost hate him. I was trying to draw the lake for you, but it turned into a sketch of my mom and dad.

Ronald showed it to the Smiths, and Mr. Smith thought I'd drawn him. He looks nothing like my dad. I felt like snatching the picture out of his hands and tearing it up in his face. But I couldn't do that. It would have hurt his feelings, and it would have been a mean thing to do. Mrs. Smith, though, thinks about things, and she knows it wasn't her and her husband.

I went outside thinking that maybe I'd try to explain things to Ronald again. He and Mr. Smith were playing basketball, and they both looked so close and seemed so happy, like a real father and son, I didn't feel like I should stay. And I knew if I stood there and kept watching, sooner or later Mr. Smith would say in his loud voice, "Come on, son, why don't you play some ball?"

He'd try and make me play, and Ronald would look at me like I was weird. I'm like a person who's nowhere, dangling in the middle of nothing.

But I will try and think positive, Doris. Getting the names of the flower shops would be impossible, though it's a good idea. I keep thinking that the last place we lived in was Manhattan, but who knows, it may have been Brooklyn. We moved around a lot since my dad was a musician and worked in different places. He wanted us to be with him wherever he made music. Ronald was very young when my parents had the car accident, and we had just moved.

Maybe I'll get some news soon. I made five more copies of the letter and the sketch the other day and

sent them out. I think you'd make a good reporter.
You ask a lot of questions. I don't mind.

Love,

Amir

P.S. I'll try again to draw you a picture of the lake.
A real nice one.

THE BRONX NEWS

Issue #1
Editor, Star Reporter, and Owner,
DORIS WILLIAMS

Wednesday, July 22nd
TODAY'S WEATHER: The Bronx is hotter
than the Sahara Desert

EDITORIAL: One Girl's Opinion

Be glad that you do not have any friends. They're
a pain most of the time. They do not want you to
have your own opinion about things, or your own
thoughts and ideas. You can't be yourself around
them but have to follow whatever they do. They even
want you to like the same people they like. They will
spread lies and gossip to turn your mind sideways so
you think stupid thoughts like they do. Without
friends, I'm free to be me.

Of course, everyone should have one true friend that you could trust with your life. It doesn't matter whether that one friend is far away and you don't get to see him in person. That's your "soul friend" and the only friend you really need. The rest are just acquaintances (people you know who don't get on your nerves) or nuisances (people you know who get on your nerves).

PERSONAL

Amir, you are truly an extra-nice, kind, wonderful human being. If I were in your sneakers, and the Smiths mistook themselves for my parents, I would have blurted out, "They're not you!" But it was nice of you not to bust everyone's bubble when they're so happy. It was only a case of mistaken identity. Just explain to Ronald that the sketch was his real mother and father. But are the Smiths fakes? To Ronald they're real as rain.

At least they're not mean to you. Why would you want to be in a group home again? Remember you said you always had to figure out ways to keep the ruffians from bothering you? At least you don't have that problem at the Smiths'. If, however, you move to a group home in the Bronx, then that would be another story. Then you wouldn't be dangling. Your two feet would be on the ground in the Bronx. My advice to you is to stay positive. Send more letters out. Say over and over: My letter will find my aunt. My aunt will find my letter.

LATE-BREAKING NEWS
By D. Williams

Charlene is becoming a very nice acquaintance of Doris's (see definitions in editorial column). They met again in the library today. "I hate double dutch," she told Doris, who was shocked. "My sisters are obsessed," she said. (She uses very big words.) The next shocking thing is that she likes to come to the library to read, because her sisters annoy her and she can't read at home. She and Doris love the same book, their all-time favorite, *Roll of Thunder, Hear My Cry*. It reminds Charlene of her grandparents down South.

Trouble in the playground again—teenagers caught selling drugs, allegedly. Charlene's sisters were on the 6 o'clock news. Not for being in trouble but for being in the background with a bunch of other kids, jumping up and down and making faces at the camera while the reporter talked about what had happened in the playground—part of a report on drugs in the city.

On a personal note, my parents are very upset about today's events, and my mother might stop working. That means she'll be home with me all day. I don't know if I'm ready for that. What an adjustment!

TOMORROW'S FORECAST: hot and boring
like today

My Dear Amir,

I guess you think I'm going crazy. But the only good
thing about today was spending time with Charlene and
creating this newspaper just for you. You gave me the
idea. Oh, by the way, you said that you all moved
around a lot to be with your father, but I thought that
your dad was away on the road playing music. I guess
you guys couldn't go on the road with him, because
then you'd miss school, right? And since Ronald was a
baby, he couldn't travel, right? Anyway, just being
curious—not nosy. Nuisances are nosy.

Your soul friend,

Doris

P.S. Did you finish the drawing of the lake yet? Here's
a tip for today. Draw a picture of Ronald like you do
for the kids at camp. I bet he'd like that.

July 27th

Dear Doris Williams, Star Reporter,

I received your letter/newspaper today. It made
me laugh and think about things, too. You should

definitely be a reporter when you grow up. You asked about my father. Sometimes he had to go on the road and we couldn't go with him. Ronald was just an infant then.

So the playground was featured on the 6 o'clock news! Is the playground that bad? I laughed when I thought about how those sisters must have looked on television. It sounds like you and Charlene are getting to be friends—or nice acquaintances, as you say. Maybe she'll be a "soul friend" one day.

Your letters are like my mom's geraniums—they make a cloudy day bright. I'm trying to be positive. My dad always used to say: "Think positive. Negative thoughts cause negative events." So I remind myself over and over that Ronald is my brother.

You reminded me of something. When I was in the group home, I used to draw pictures of the kids there, and I would make some of the ruffians look so handsome, they were real nice to me. I took your advice and tried the same thing with Ronald.

I drew a picture of the lake and I put him swimming in it, even though he can't swim. He liked it more than I thought he would. While I was drawing him, I was thinking of a way to talk to him about his true family. And his real mother and father. But he was so excited sitting next to me on the bench and watching me draw, and even giving me helpful hints like "Amir, you made the water too wavy." Or "Amir, you made me too small." Then he stood up and started posing as if he was swimming. He makes me laugh sometimes. I didn't want to see that blank look on his face when I talked about our real parents, so I didn't say anything. I'll wait for the right time.

Anyway, I was going to give you the picture of Ronald swimming in the lake, but he wanted it, so I let him keep it. He's been showing it to his friends like it was a photograph and he was really swimming. Haven't gotten any answers yet from the letters I sent out. Mr. Smith thinks my aunt may have moved to another state. I hope not. I hope she lives in the Bronx or Manhattan—even Brooklyn or Queens would be better than another state.

Answer soon.

Love,

Amir

P.S. I promise—you will get a picture of the lake.

2 P.M.
Friday
July 31st

My Dear Amir,

I hope that you are very fine—just like the sugar.

I wait patiently for my picture. Put me swimming in the lake, too. Be sure and make my arms very long— to answer your question before you ask it, no, I do not know how to swim. I don't blame you for giving Ronald the drawing of himself swimming. Your drawings are like magic to him. You can make him be anything he wants to be.

I've been thinking over what you said in your letter about telling Ronald about his real family. I guess you could say Ronald has his real family— the Smiths and you. Remember I told you about friends—soul friends and acquaintances. Family is like that too. Here's what I've been thinking: There's blood family and chosen family.

Blood family is the people you are related to by blood—all of y'all look alike. Maybe everyone in the family has a square head or something. Like I am tall like my father's side of the family. Chosen family is like soul friends. People who really take care of each other even if they don't have to. The Smiths could send you and Ronald back to foster care if they wanted to. Now, the best thing is if you have blood and chosen family all in one—like me and my mother and father and Gerald (sometimes). But then again, maybe it doesn't even matter.

When you find your aunt, everything will be perfect and Ronald will understand and your blood family and chosen family will be one. That's *One Girl's Opinion.*

My mother calmed down and will continue working. To tell the truth, even though Gerald is a pest, I like being the boss of the house and taking care of him until she gets home. My father is threatening to move us. But he's always been talking about buying a house and moving someday. I can't imagine living anywhere else but 163rd Street—I don't think I want to live anywhere else until I grow up.

The block association and some other people in the neighborhood are getting together to "Take the Playground Back." Everyone got all worked up—said the television news programs only come to our neighborhood to report bad things and would never report anything good.

Well, I'm going to change all that. The next issue of my paper will only have good news. I think I would like to be a reporter, but I'll only report the good stuff. I'm working on a new issue of The Bronx News. Guess I missed my deadline. If I don't do better, I'll have to fire myself.

I ran into Charlene again this morning in the library. She's baby-sitting her sister Claudette like I have to baby-sit Gerald. Seems like her sisters have made her the one who always has to baby-sit. We read together while we waited for storytime to finish. As we read, Charlene changed right before my eyes. She lost her sad face and it was like she became a character in the story. Listening to her read was like watching television almost. She made the story so alive that I stopped noticing that her cornrows needed redoing.

Then Charlene said she had to go to the playground because she didn't want her sisters coming to the library looking for her. "All they think about is double dutch and being in first place in that double-dutch tournament in the fall." I thought to myself how terrible it must be to have bossy, loony sisters bugging you all the time. It makes me appreciate Gerald. At least in his world I'm the boss.

Anyway, me and Charlene have a lot in common. She might even become a soul friend, like you. We're going to meet in the library again tomorrow. Also, she's coming around the block to visit me later on— I'm not allowed to have company when my parents aren't home. So we'll just sit on the stoop in front of my building. I know the rumor factory will be working overtime—Doris is hanging out with those drugged-up sisters, Doris is getting wild, Doris is doing . . . You know the rest. They better not say it, otherwise I will be going upside some heads—starting with Lavinia and the twins.

Only one month more of summer vacation, and then a whole new world of middle school. I can't wait. It'll be so nice to get away from all of my immature ex-friends.

Well, I guess that's all for now. Gerald just woke

up, and Charlene just rang the downstairs bell. Bye
for now.

Love,

Doris
Your one true friend

Amir folded Doris's letter and put it in his pocket.
Though he was sitting on the bench in the backyard,
he hadn't heard the car coming up the driveway.

Ronald's voice startled him. "Mama and Papa
bought you a paint set and two sketchpads."

Alvin Smith slammed the car door and frowned.
"Boy, you like a broken refrigerator. Can't hold nothing."

Mrs. Smith shook her head. "Ronald, we wanted
to surprise Amir."

"He is surprised. Ain't you surprised, Amir?" He
smiled earnestly at his brother.

Amir stood up, looking more confused than
surprised. "Thank you," he stammered. "I . . . uh . . .
I . . . I really appreciate this."

Mr. Smith handed Amir a large package. "Now you
can finish that drawing of me and Mama here, son."

Amir nodded but didn't flinch.

"Alvin, don't worry the boy, telling him what to
paint."

"He's going to paint me, right, Amir?" Ronald looked up at him.

"Ronald, you, too. Stop worrying your brother. He'll paint what he wants when he wants," Mrs. Smith said.

"Thank you," Amir repeated, and his eyes opened wide when he pulled up the lid of the large aluminum case. Inside were colored pencils and markers—shades of red, purple, tan, brown—cakes of watercolors, oil pastels, drawing pencils, paintbrushes, a mixing tray, and a pencil sharpener and eraser. He was speechless.

Ronald tugged at Amir's shirtsleeve. "Come on, Amir, paint a picture of me."

"Boy, you think the sun rises and sets on you," Mr. Smith said. "Amir is going to finish the picture of me and your mother." He fingered his mustache. "Going to put some color on our faces. Because we are people of color, you know."

Mrs. Smith giggled. "Hush your foolishness. *Now* where is the sun rising and setting? You and Ronald are like two peas in a pod. Leave Amir alone."

Alvin studied Amir for a moment. "Do you really like the paint set?"

"Yes, sir. I do."

Ronald tugged at Amir's sleeve again, "So you going to paint a picture of me now?"

"Okay, okay, I'll paint a picture of you."

Mr. Smith folded his thick arms. "I think me and your mama spoiled you, Ronald."

Grace rubbed Ronald's head. "He's a sweet kid. Not spoiled, just pampered and treasured, the way all children should be."

"That's right, Mama. I'm not spoiled. Come on, Amir, paint my picture." He pulled Amir toward the bench as the Smiths went into the house.

Ronald and Amir sat facing each other, and Amir began sketching out Ronald's round face. He was surprised that Ronald sat so still. He didn't begin to fidget until Amir was almost finished. As his drawing came to life, Amir recognized traces of familiar images in Ronald's face—his nose with gracefully flaring nostrils and his deep dimples. Amir's heart raced, and he put his pencil down. "You tired now?" he asked Ronald.

"No. Let me see how I look."

"When I'm finished. Don't you want to take a break?"

Ronald reached for the sketch. "No. I want to see it."

Bruce, one of Ronald's friends, walked into the yard just then. For the moment the sketch was forgotten as Ronald jumped off the bench and ran over to his friend. Amir was relieved. He went upstairs and took several pieces of paper out of his notebook.

Saturday

August 8th

Dear Doris,

I hope everything is okay. Your last letter made me laugh, but think about things, too. Soul family and chosen family. Maybe that's why I didn't get annoyed when Mr. Smith called me "son" just now. I hardly noticed it. Part of it could've been because the Smiths bought me a fantastic paint set and new sketchpads today, and I was so surprised, I could hardly say thank you. I was touched and shocked. Almost speechless. I hope they don't think I'm ungrateful. No foster parents have ever done such a nice thing for me.

I've always dreamed about having a set like this. Then when Mr. Smith started talking about finishing the picture of them—the one they think is them—it didn't make me angry like before; maybe a little annoyed. I keep reminding myself that he's only trying to be nice. I'll surprise them with a drawing of themselves.

Ronald was as excited as if the gift had been for him. Some kids would've been jealous. When I think about it, he's like that, even with his friends. He shares whatever he has. I guess the Smiths taught him that. My parents taught us the same thing. As I drew Ronald, I began to see how much he looks like our mother and father all wrapped up in one little boy. I had to take a break.

Doris, you will have to fire yourself if you don't get your paper out on time. I think it's nice that you and Charlene are hanging out. It's hard enough being different from your friends; it's even harder when you're different from your own brothers and sisters. Seems to me that you and Charlene are more alike than Charlene and her own sisters.

What about everyone else? Yellow Bird, Big Russell, Lavinia, and the twins? Guess you guys still haven't made up? One day the twins will realize that you're a good friend. About those drug rumors—I wouldn't even listen to them.

Oh, by the way, I still haven't heard from anyone answering the letters. Only one came back; it said "addressee unknown."

I guess that's all for now. Ronald is downstairs calling for me to finish his drawing. Now I can make you a beautiful painting of the lake, too.

Love,

Amir

P.S. Only three weeks left of day camp. I was nominated for the best counselor award. Imagine that!

As Amir finished his letter, Ronald burst into the room.

"You finished the painting yet?"

"No."

"Well, can you finish it now?"

"Okay."

"Let's go outside."

"Why? I can finish here."

"I like it outside. Let's sit on the bench like we was doing."

Amir glanced out the window. The light was changing, and the beginnings of an orange-reddish tinge slowly colored the sky. "Okay, we'll go outside."

Beaming, Ronald dashed down the stairs and was out the door by the time Amir reached the kitchen.

Amir colored in Ronald's face using a bronze-tone pencil—his coloring, too, was exactly like their mother's. Amir tried once again to say something about her and their father, but the words didn't sound right in his head and couldn't reach his tongue. Ronald sat next to him like the perfect model with a huge smile on his face.

Amir chuckled. "Ronald, you're going to hurt your face if you keep smiling like that."

When Amir finished, the sun was about to set. Ronald ran to Mr. and Mrs. Smith with the drawing.

Mr. Smith turned to Amir. "You are truly talented, son," he said.

"Thank you," Amir answered, remembering not to say sir.

Ronald rushed upstairs with the drawing. "Where are you going?" Alvin asked.

"I'm gonna hang it up."

Amir ran after him. "No, wait. I'll buy a frame for it when I get paid."

"No. I like it the way it is." Ronald pulled off his sneakers, jumped on the bed, and quickly taped the picture to the wall, next to the one of him swimming in the lake. He stepped back to see whether it was crooked and almost fell off the bed as he was backing away. Amir caught him, and they both tumbled to the floor. They laughed together for the first time since Amir had been living there. Ronald's chuckling and giggling reminded Amir of his other brothers and sisters. In this moment the memory didn't hurt.

When Amir returned home from camp the next day, he checked the mailbox as he always did before entering the yard. He found the usual bills and letters. He had two letters from Doris and a return of another of the letters he'd sent out—addressee unknown.

He walked around to the back of the house wondering why Doris had written him twice. *Must be some rocking news in the Bronx.* He was disappointed, though, that he had received another addressee-unknown return.

When Amir walked into the yard, Ronald stopped playing basketball and ran over to him. "Amir, draw a picture of me and Bruce."

"In a minute," Amir said, surprised that Ronald had seen him entering the yard. He rarely noticed anyone when he was shooting hoops. "Let me go in the house first. I have something to do."

"What do you have to do?"

"Something. It won't take long. I'll be right back."

Amir opened the screen door and quickly stepped into the kitchen. Ronald was at his heels.

"You left Bruce out there alone," Amir reminded him.

"I know. That's why you have to draw us now. Bruce been here all day waiting for you. He has to go home soon."

"He can't wait five minutes more?"

"No, Amir. Please?" Ronald whined.

Grace Smith waved to them as she talked on the telephone, and Amir handed her the mail. Ronald's sharp round eyes glanced at the other letters, which Amir put in his backpack.

Amir ran up the stairs, but Ronald raced ahead of him. He plopped himself on the top step and folded his arms as if he were blocking Amir. "What do you have to do now?" Ronald asked.

"I told you I'll be right down. You sure treat your friends bad, leaving Bruce alone like that." He gently moved Ronald out of his way and entered the bedroom. Ronald followed.

"Who wrote you letters, Amir?"

"My friend, Doris."

"Your girlfriend?"

"No. She's not my girlfriend. Where you get that idea from?" Amir rested his bag on the bed.

Ronald's eyes twinkled as he sat on the side of Amir's bed. "You just want to read your girlfriend's letters."

"I told you she's not my girlfriend."

"She's always writing you letters and saying nice things to you."

Amir's mouth flew open in surprise. "You been reading my letters?"

Ronald grinned. "No, I can't read her letters. She uses too many big words."

Amir opened the drawer where he kept his letters and started stuffing them into his backpack. "It's not right, Ronald. You're not supposed to read other people's private mail. I can't believe you did that."

"Gotcha!" Ronald lay across the bed as laughter bubbled out of him. "I didn't read your old letters from your girlfriend, but I see you reading them over and over, and . . ."

Amir sighed and pulled Ronald off the bed. "You're like a little ant in my pants. Come on, I'll draw you and Bruce. You sure you ain't been reading my letters?"

"I hate to read," Ronald said as he dashed out of the room.

Ronald and Bruce had already started playing ball again when Amir came outside and sat down on the bench. He adjusted his sketchpad till it was comfortable on his lap and watched them playing basketball—jumping as high as their short legs would allow. Ronald was spinning and dribbling like he'd seen the stars do on television. As Amir watched them, he began to sketch. He drew their legs and arms very long, so that they seemed to be stretching way above their heads to the sky.

Then he drew buildings and fire escapes and a milk crate with no bottom tied to one of the fire escape rungs. However, the game ended when Bruce's mother called him home, shouting his name from the next yard.

Ronald bounced toward Amir and peeped over his shoulder. He pointed at the drawing and laughed. "This ain't me and Bruce. Who are these people you drawing? Where is this?"

"Where I used to live, in the city," Amir said. "A Hundred and Sixty-third Street in the Bronx. These were some of the guys who used to play basketball. I'm going to put you and Bruce in this neighborhood. It'll be like you took a trip."

Ronald's eyes grew wide. "Yeah? What's their names?"

"Yellow Bird, Big Russell."

"They play as good as me and Bruce? Their legs that long?" he asked in amazement.

Amir smiled. "That's just a style of art. They're older than you and Bruce, so they have more experience playing."

"What kind of hoop is that?"

"A milk crate that they made a basket out of."

"That's stupid. Draw a picture of me playing ball. Just me, and make my legs and arms long like that."

"What about Bruce?"

"Draw him tomorrow."

Amir smiled. "Okay. You know our mother and father and all of us used to live in the city."

"How come you don't play ball?" Ronald asked, skipping around Amir's comment.

Amir wondered how many times Ronald would ask him the same question. "I never learned how."

"Why didn't you learn how? Why didn't Yellow Bird and Big Russell teach you?"

"I don't know why I never learned. I wasn't good at it. Right now I'm trying to draw you playing ball like you asked me to."

"Make my legs look real long. And draw me doing this."

Amir had a hard time drawing because Ronald was making him laugh so much as he spun, twirled, and dribbled, leaping as high as he could.

Amir drew a little boy with elongated arms and legs reaching for a basket as high as the sun. He turned the sun into a bright red-orange ball and drew silhouettes of Ronald in various moves and positions.

Amir sketched quickly and intensely, now that he had his design in mind. He felt as though he was inside his own drawing—bolting, leaping, hurtling, and flying with Ronald. Time flew as well. Amir didn't even hear Mr. Smith drive up and put his car in the garage.

Memories

Mr. Smith walked into the yard shouting his familiar greeting, "Hey, everybody, Big Papa's in the house."

Ronald dropped his basketball and ran over to him. "You mean in the yard, Papa."

Amir looked up from his drawing and smiled. "Hi, Mister Alvin," he said, forgetting to say sir or Mr. Smith.

Alvin Smith threw his large head back and laughed loudly. So did Ronald, though he didn't know what he was laughing at. Grace Smith opened the screen door. "Let me in on the joke, too," she said, kissing her husband lightly on the cheek.

"Boy, Amir just said something that I haven't heard since I was a kid in the South. He called me Mister Alvin. We used to call all the grownups Miss or Mister." His wide face grew even wider as he grinned and bowed, tipping an imaginary hat. "'Good morning, Miss Idabellmae,' we'd say, or 'Good afternoon, Mister Charlie,' or 'How do, Miss Grace.'"

His wife tapped him playfully on the arm. "Go on with your foolishness." She saw how embarrassed Amir looked and hushed her husband, who was still chuckling and laughing.

She turned to Amir. "Your parents taught you to say that?"

Amir nodded, feeling confused, not sure if he sounded ridiculous. Or if he'd said something wrong.

"It just slipped out. My mother used to tell us that if there are adults you feel close to, it's okay to say their first name, but you had to put a title to it. Out of respect."

Grace put her arm around Amir's shoulder. "That's right. I had to do the same thing in Ohio."

Alvin took out his handkerchief and wiped his sweaty face. Pieces of cement still stuck to his hands. "Well, son, that's better than sir or Mr. Smith." He grinned and bowed again to his wife. "I guess you'll be calling Mama here Miss Grace." He turned in Amir's direction. "I hope you don't think I was laughing at you, son. It just brought back some good old down-home memories. You all right?"

"Yes, sir . . . I mean Mister Alvin."

"Still can't say Pops, huh?"

Grace pulled her husband's shirtsleeve and headed for the house. "In the fullness of time," she said.

Amir didn't know what she meant. But it didn't matter. He also wondered why he'd said Mister Alvin, but that didn't matter, either. It felt right and comfortable. He'd wait until after supper, when everyone else was in the living room watching television, before going upstairs to read and enjoy Doris's two letters.

THE BRONX NEWS

Issue #2

(The Good News Issue)

Editor, Star Reporter, and Owner,

DORIS WILLIAMS

Thursday, August 13th

TODAY'S WEATHER: *HOT, HOT, HOT*

EDITORIAL: One Girl's Opinion

Rumors and gossip are like viruses. They all make you sick. People who spread rumors are like walking infections. The lying words from their mouths spread like disease from person to person. The only way to stop the disease is to keep your mouth shut. I refuse to repeat a rumor even though it's about a good acquaintance of mine and her sisters. She would feel terrible if she knew what people were saying. I think we should make the people we like feel good and not hurt their feelings by telling them something we heard someone say about them.

I know I'm right about this. How do I know? I put myself in the other person's sneakers, and then I follow one of my parents' constant sayings: "Do unto others as you would have them do unto you." Follow this and good news will follow you.

BREAKING NEWS
By D. Williams

Last Monday morning while the fabulous and wonderful Doris and Charlene were sitting near the large window in the library reading *Roll of Thunder, Hear My Cry* together, they heard loud thumping on the library window. They turned around and saw Charlene's sisters with their noses pressed to the window, looking like Disney on Parade.

When they started shouting for Charlene to come outside, the librarian rushed to the door. Charlene was embarrassed and fought back tears. "See what I mean, Doris?" she said, "They're trying to make me do what they want me to do."

A humiliated Charlene gave up. She returned the book and got her baby sister, who started crying because she didn't want to leave storytime. Together they dashed out of the library. Why all the ruckus? Charlene's sisters wanted her to practice double dutch with them.

Doris feels like crying for Charlene, too, and is glad that she doesn't have any sisters. Doris didn't see Charlene for the rest of the week. Each day she went to the library expecting her to be there. She even walked over to Charlene's block one day to look for her, but she didn't find her.

On Saturday Doris got a big surprise when Charlene came to visit her by herself. She didn't have to baby-sit. The girls had a nice time sipping lemonade and eating cupcakes. Charlene was happy because her sisters couldn't find her as long as she was in Doris's house. Charlene told Doris that she stayed away from the library all week because she didn't want her sisters to follow her there and embarrass her again.

OTHER NEWS

Lavinia and the twins spoke to Doris yesterday for the first time in weeks. "You don't care who you hang out with, do you?" Lavinia asked.

Doris answered, "Yes, I do. That's why I don't hang out with you." She threw her head up in the air and kept on stepping down the street. The friendship seems to be over forever. This is good news.

One of the neighbors gave Yellow Bird and Big Russell a real basketball hoop. This is the best news.

ADVERTISEMENTS

Wanted: One drawing of a lake

OBITUARY

A sad note that must be reported. The Beauty Hive has closed. Miss Bee could no longer afford the high rent. D. Williams will miss her job and the people there.

My Dear Amir,

I hope you like this latest issue of The Bronx News. Guess you must think I'm really tripping. You could say, too, that Charlene and I are becoming real friends and not just acquaintances. To tell you the truth, I don't mind having a good friend close by. If anyone needs a friend, Charlene does.

She promised to meet me in the library tomorrow. I told her that I didn't judge her by her sisters. She was still my friend. She said that she loves to read because reading takes her away from her life. Isn't that a strange thing to say? I like to read too and escape, but not from my life.

"At least you have your sisters," I told her. "I know someone who wishes he was with his brothers and sisters."

I thought about you, Amir, and how much you want to find your family. But suppose you're different from them? They are still your family, and I guess that's what counts. I don't believe that Charlene dislikes her sisters as much as she says she does. She's just different from them.

You and Ronald are different, too, but I bet he's glad that you're a kind big brother to him. You paint his picture, which means I can't get my drawing of the lake—just joking. Anyway, Ronald is lucky, and I hope when you find the others that you all get along good, too.

Before you know it, school will be starting. Fortunately Charlene and I will be in the same class—the top class, of course. Are you nervous about going to high school? All those humongous teenagers. Just keep drawing (smile).

Bye for now.

Love,

Doris

P.S. If you're not voted the best counselor, then there's something wrong with the judges.

The sounds of the television downstairs, and Mister Alvin and Ronald both shouting over the baseball game they were watching, faded in the background as Amir carefully folded Doris's newspaper and letter in two and put them in his backpack—just in case Ronald got curious. He opened the second letter, expecting to be transported to the Bronx again.

11 P.M.
Friday
August 14th

My Dear Amir,

A night breeze just blew into the Bronx. You're

probably wondering why I'm writing you so soon, and why I'm writing a letter instead of a newspaper. The answer to those questions is this is no time for silliness. Maybe you didn't even get the newspaper and letter I sent you yesterday. I'm writing you now because I can't sleep. And I can't sleep because I keep thinking about a very shocking thing that happened today. I don't know what to do, and I don't have anyone else to talk to except you.

Charlene was already at the library when I got there this morning. She looked like she'd been crying.

"What's wrong with you?" I asked her.

"My sisters," she whispered, her bottom lip trembling.

"What did they do to you now?" I asked her.

"They don't want me to be friends with you."

"Why?"

"They say you're a bad influence on me."

That made me angry. "How could I be a bad influence on you? I don't fight, play hookey, or *do drugs*," I blurted out. My mom always tells me to put a lock on my tongue before the wrong words escape. I was immediately sorry, but it was too late.

Charlene looked surprised, hurt, scared, and then angry, too. "Nobody said anything about drugs, Doris. Why'd you bring up drugs? My sisters said you're turning me into a nerd. They say that I'm trying to act corny like you."

I was still ashamed over what I'd said about drugs. "Tell your sisters you're being yourself. You're not trying to act like anybody. Stand up to them," I said.

Charlene's lips continued to tremble and tears rolled slowly down her face. "I do stand up to them. Then we end up fighting and my mother starts blaming me because she says we're all family and I shouldn't act uppity with my own sisters. I just want to be myself. I don't see why I have to do everything they do." She wiped her face with the corner of her T-shirt, but the tears kept flowing. "I hate double dutch and I hate my life. I can't even read in peace at home."

I was shocked because how can you hate the only life you have? "But they were happy for you when you won the award," I said.

"They just wanted to jump up and down and make a spectacle of themselves and embarrass me."

Suddenly I wondered whether the drug rumors I'd been hearing all summer were true. Maybe that's the real problem and Charlene can't talk about it. I had to go back on my word and tell her.

"I'm not starting rumors," I said, "but we're friends. That's why I'm telling you what people are saying." It was so hard for me to say it, but I finally forced the words out. "People are saying that your sisters do drugs."

She wiped her eyes and her face with the back of her hand. "Friends always tell each other the truth and trust each other with secrets, right?"

I nodded, because by this time I could hardly talk myself. You know I can't stand to see a friend crying or hurting. It makes a big lump clog up my own throat.

"The truth is my sisters don't do drugs, and I don't either," Charlene said. "Marijuana is a plant." At first I didn't know what she was talking about. She dug in her jeans pocket and showed me what looked like a cigarette butt. But I knew it wasn't a cigarette. I guess I gasped so loud, she thought I was choking. The librarian glared at us.

"Come on outside, Doris, while the kids are in storytime." She pulled my arm, and I followed her. I asked her whether she was holding the marijuana for her sisters, and she said, "No. It's mine."

"You said we'd always be honest with each other, Charlene. I think you're lying. Now I know why you say you hate your sisters. They're making you do drugs."

"Doris, you're being naive." She'd stopped crying and seemed like her old, grownup-sounding self.

"You need to throw that junk away," I warned her.

"I told you, marijuana is not drugs; it's a plant," she said. "People use it for medicinal purposes."

"Are you sick?" I asked.

"I've only tried it a few times," she said. "When I

smoke it, my sisters don't get on my nerves. Why don't you try it? Then you'll see. There's nothing to it."

"Nobody's getting on my nerves that bad. Why do you let your sisters rule you? Tell your mother what they're doing."

All of a sudden it seemed like she got mad. "My sisters don't smoke marijuana and they don't know I've tried it." Then she held out her hand like some kind of offering. "Why don't you try it? It makes Third Avenue look nice, and it's not a drug."

I shook my head. "If your sisters didn't give it to you, then where did you get it from?"

"T.T."

"T.T.?" I nearly fainted. "How could you hang with him?"

"I'm not hanging with him," she said. "He lives in my building."

"But it's junk," I said. "That's why they call drug addicts junkies."

"You're very extreme, Doris. This is not the same as taking drugs."

For a minute I wondered what it felt like. Then I didn't want to know, because I remembered what my mother's hands felt like going upside my head.

Of all the sisters, Charlene was the last one I ever thought would be messing with pot. And with T.T., a sixth-grade reject.

I tried to get her to throw the butt away, but she

wouldn't. Said she'd flush it down the toilet when she got home. Said she didn't want to throw it away in front of the library. I knew that was a lie.

Then she looked guilty and sad. "Doris, you're the only real friend I have. Please don't tell anyone. Please don't get me in trouble."

"I won't," I said. "I'd never get you in trouble. You're getting your own self in trouble if you don't stop."

I know I promised Charlene that I wouldn't say anything, and I'm only telling you, Amir, because I'm sure you won't repeat this story. And everyone knows anyway. It's terrible when a bad rumor about a friend turns out to be true.

In a way I feel like Charlene betrayed me. But I still feel bad for her. How could someone so smart act so stupid? I will stay by myself from now on. You must promise me, Amir, that we'll be friends forever, because I can't trust anyone else.

Everything is changing around me.
I had a friend, lost a friend.
Will the loneliness never end?
My one true friend is so far away,
But we'll meet again some fine day.

Good night, Amir,

Doris

Amir stared blankly at the letter for a moment, his mouth slightly open. The space he occupied and the familiar sounds of the house were no longer there. He felt stupid. He was overreacting, he knew, but he couldn't help it.

Doris's letter had called up all the old memories he'd been trying to bury. They spilled out of the hidden places in his heart and stood before him. The sadness that he'd kept locked in that small corner of his brain broke loose and captured his spirit.

He began to fold the second letter until it was a small square that fit in the palm of his hand.

Ronald burst into the room. "Amir, Amir, guess who won the ball game!"

Amir hardly noticed him. His voice seemed very far away.

"What's wrong with you, Amir?"

"Nothing."

"You look like you sick. You sick? I'll tell Mama."

Amir grabbed Ronald's arm before he bolted out of the room. "I'm not sick. Don't bother your mother." He realized that he'd never before referred to Grace as Ronald's mother. "I'm okay. Don't worry Miss Grace."

The sounds of the television drifted up to him. Ronald had brought the world back. "You're supposed to be going to bed now, right?"

Ronald's sharp eyes searched Amir's face. "Why

you so sad? You want to draw a picture of me? I'll sit quiet if you want to draw me again."

"No. You just go to sleep. I'm going, too."

But Amir could not sleep. The bad memories rode him like the old hag in the ghost stories his mother used to tell him. When he heard Ronald snoring lightly, he eased out of his bed. He turned on the dim end-table lamp and ripped a blank piece of paper out of his notebook.

1 A.M.
Thursday morning
August 20th

Dear Doris,

I received both of your letters this afternoon when I came in from camp. When I read the first one, I was laughing and enjoyed The Bronx News and was happy that you had found a friend to hang out with. But your second letter shocked me. It made me feel very bad and reminded me of a lot of things I try to forget . . .

Amir stopped writing. Could she understand? How would the shameful memories look written down in black and white for Doris to see? He put the paper in his backpack, lay back down, and turned off the light. If he kept the normal night-time sounds in his head, then perhaps he wouldn't be pulled back to a place that he never wanted to return to again. He heard Ronald snoring, his own heart pumping, crickets chirping. His mind latched onto every sound, listening for every little creak and crack in the walls and the floorboards.

He got up again and turned the lamp back on. He tore the unfinished letter into tiny pieces and reached for his sketchpad. Ronald turned over but didn't wake up. Amir began to draw a flower. He painstakingly drew and colored the scalloped edges of the dark green leaves and every small red petal. His mother's geraniums brightening their small, sad world. After the last red petal was colored in, he was able to fall asleep.

10 A.M.
Monday
August 24th

My Dear Amir,

How are you? Are you sick or something? I'm okay, I guess. The sky has turned into an ocean. Me and Gerald couldn't go to the library this morning. I wanted to write you a little note while I'm waiting for this rain to stop. If it doesn't end soon, me and Gerald will drive each other crazy. When I'm in the mood again and something good happens around here, I'll send you another Bronx News.

I hope that you received my last two letters. I'm anxious to know what you think about Charlene. I haven't seen her since she told me her secret. She stopped coming to the library, so now I just hang out with me, myself, and Gerald. I feel sorry for Charlene, but I'm angry with her, too.

If Charlene doesn't have sense enough to tell her mother about her sisters, then that's her problem. I can't even picture her hanging out with T.T., smoking pot. He doesn't come around here anymore. Maybe she was lying to me about him, because she doesn't want to tell on her sisters.

Lavinia and the twins were right for the first time in their lives, and maybe I should apologize to them. But I still don't like their attitude.

Gerald is bugging me as I write. He is pulling my arm and whining, "Dawiss, libree." I'll have to read him a story. That's the only thing that will settle him down when he gets like this. Have to go now.

Write soon!

Your soul friend,

Doris

P.S. Are you still sending out letters?

"Amir!" Ronald screeched from the bottom of the stairs just as Amir finished reading Doris's letter. "It's family devotional time," he yelled, almost like a taunt, as if he knew his brother didn't want to sit through family devotions.

Amir walked slowly down the stairs. Alvin sank back into his recliner that over the years had taken the shape of his broad frame. Grace sat on the sofa, and Ronald was sprawled on the floor in front of the blank television screen.

Alvin smiled as if something special was about to happen. "Son, I just heard from my cousin that he found out where your uncle worked. The owner of the place said he moved to Virginia with his family. So Max is going to make some calls down there."

Grace sucked her teeth. "Alvin, I thought you said we'd wait until we knew for sure. We don't even know where in Virginia."

"I'm just keeping Amir updated. He's got to be hopeful."

Amir nodded. "Yes, sir, I'm hopeful."

Alvin frowned at him. "You don't sound hopeful. What happened to Mister Alvin? Son, is there something bothering you? If so, now is the time to speak on it."

"Nothing's bothering me. . . . I . . . Nothing. I'm fine."

"Well, aren't you excited that we found out

where your aunt and her husband are?" Alvin's voice rose slightly in frustration.

"I'm happy that you're close to finding them," Amir mumbled.

Grace cleared her throat. "Sit here, Amir." She made space for him next to her on the couch. "Alvin, maybe this is not the time."

"But this is our family devotions. We're here to help one another. Amir, talk to us."

"I'm okay, Mister Alvin," he said, trying to sound regular and normal.

Alvin shook his head slightly. "Amir, I might not be a well-educated person, but I'm a feeling person, and I can tell that something is worrying you." He leaned forward and stared directly at Amir. "It seemed like you were beginning to settle in; now all of a sudden we're back to square one. What is troubling you, son?"

Amir lowered his eyes and didn't answer. He could not begin to tell Mr. Smith what had happened to him.

Ronald jumped up from the floor. "Amir is in trouble?"

"No, Ronald," Grace said. "Troubling means something is worrying you."

Ronald started dribbling his imaginary basketball around the living room. Then he held the ball to his chest and made faces as if someone was trying to grab it.

"Ronald!" the Smiths yelled at the same time.

Alvin reached for him. "Boy, is you crazy?"

"I'm just trying to make Amir happy. Make him laugh."

"I'm not unhappy, Ronald." Amir was touched by his brother's efforts to cheer him up, and he tried to smile for Ronald's sake.

"Well, let me tell you what's bothering me," Alvin said. "It bothers me when we don't trust each other. When things worry us, we can't be afraid to say what they are. We're a family here."

Grace said, "Nothing's bothering me except I want to see Ronald play less basketball and read more this coming school year." She stared at Ronald, who'd been making faces at himself in the television screen. "You hear me, Ronald? What's bothering you?"

"I want to look at television."

"Guess that means that nothing's bothering him," Alvin said.

Grace looked exasperated. "Well, then, let's go to the positive things we are happy about and thankful for. Ronald, we'll start with you."

Amir wanted to stand up, shout, "I don't want to do this," and storm out of the room. But that was not his way, so he sat quietly and tried to concentrate on listening to Ronald.

"So, Ronald. Is there anything you want to say?" Grace asked. "Something that made you happy this week?"

"I beat Bruce every game we played."

Alvin rubbed his mustache. "But what else, my man? Would you be mad if he won and you lost?"

"Yeah."

"He wouldn't be your friend because he won?" Grace asked.

"Well, yeah, sometimes he wins—but I still would be mad because I lost."

"Suppose you lost Bruce. Suppose he got mad at you and didn't want to be your friend. Would you be happy then?" Alvin leaned back in his recliner.

Ronald thought for a moment, twisting one leg around the other. "No, but I'd be glad that I won the game."

"Well, think about this, Ronald," Grace said. "Suppose you always won, and Bruce and your other friends got angry with you. So angry that they didn't want to play with you. How would you feel?"

"Bad."

Alvin said, "So what do you think is the most important thing? Winning all of the games or losing a friend?"

Ronald looked confused. "Losing a friend?" he asked, not sure of the answer.

"You got it," Alvin said.

Grace nodded. "That's right, it's the friendship. So you should be thankful for Bruce's friendship, which has nothing to do with who wins or who loses a game. The friendship is the most important thing." She clasped her hands and said, "Now, let me tell you what I'm thankful for."

Amir didn't listen. He was still hearing her previous words: *The friendship is the most important thing.* Then he remembered what his mother often said: *A true friendship doesn't break easy.*

"Amir, it's your turn—what are you thankful for?" Ronald tugged at his shirtsleeve.

"Friendship."

He didn't even have to look at Grace and Alvin to sense their disappointment. He knew they hoped he'd say family. "And I won the best counselor award," he added, to change the subject.

"You didn't even mention it." Grace sounded a little hurt.

"I just found out today, and I was saving it for now to tell you."

Alvin stood up. "That's wonderful. I could tell you were good with kids. Now, once again, is there anything bothering us that we want to speak on?" He looked around the room as though he was talking to everyone, but Amir knew better.

"No, Mister Alvin. Nothing." He wondered, as he listened to Alvin's voice saying a prayer, whether the Smiths knew the whole story about him and Ronald, and their parents, too.

"Dear Lord, thank you for your many blessings …"

Amir kept thinking: *A true friendship doesn't break easy.*

Amir went straight to his room after the family devotions ended. He was afraid Alvin would follow him upstairs and try to talk to him, so he was relieved when the telephone rang and he heard Alvin laughing and talking to someone on the other end. The television suddenly blared; Ronald must have turned it on. Amir sat on the side of his bed and opened his notebook to a clean page. He wrote quickly and let the truth pour out.

Friday evening
August 28th

Dear Doris,

I am sorry I took so long to write you back. I received all of your letters and The Bronx News. Your newspaper as always is great, but your letters about Charlene made me feel real bad. They brought back some terrible memories. I think you should tell her mother about her and her sisters. You said she was your good acquaintance, but I think she is your friend, and you might be the only person who can help her. "A true friendship doesn't break easy," my mother used to say. I hope you believe that.

Suppose you found out something about me like you found out about Charlene. Would you abandon me? Would you still be my one true friend? Or would you break the friendship like it was a piece of glass? Doris, I've been wanting to tell you some things for a long time—even before I left the Bronx—but I couldn't. I was afraid you'd look down on me. Or hate me.

Your letter about Charlene brought back bad memories that I'd sealed up and buried deep inside myself. Now it's like the seal on the box has broken, and bad memories are spilling all over me. I want to tell you about them, but I am ashamed. Sometimes I wonder what's the point of telling anyhow, but maybe it will make me feel better. Like one of my counselors used to say, "There are times when you need to talk things out."

Ronald always asks me why I don't play basketball. I couldn't really tell him why; I didn't want to think about it, or talk about it. Instead, I told him the same stories I told you about our mother and father. He didn't want to listen, and I guess he was right because I wasn't going to tell him the whole story anyhow. I think you suspected, too, that my story wasn't complete. That's why you kept asking me questions about my father and my parents' accident.

The reason I don't play basketball, baseball, or any other kind of ball is because I never learned how to play.

And the reason I never learned how to play is because I was always busy. All those stories I told you about my parents and the things they said to us and the fun times we had were true, but I didn't tell you the other side— when things began to change. That happened when I was about eight or nine years old.

First, my father got sick. But it wasn't a hospital or doctor kind of sick. He stopped playing music.

My mother stopped growing her geraniums and making pretty dresses for my sisters. She started working in a factory, and then in a restaurant after the factory closed.

We moved around a lot because after a while my father couldn't work—not because he was a musician, like I told you. He was too sick to work, so my parents kept moving to find cheaper places to live. Each new place was worse than the one before.

My mother, though, enrolled us in school, and I made sure we got there. My mom and dad insisted on that. Neither of them wanted truant officers and other people coming around asking why we weren't in school.

I was perfect in every school I attended because I didn't want anyone asking me questions. Also, I didn't want my mom and dad to get in trouble, and it was warm in school—not freezing like in some of the places we lived in. I got free breakfast and lunch, too.

The other kids always looked at me funny when

I first went to a new school. Guess I was funny-
looking—like Charlene and her sisters. But I'd draw
good pictures and give them away. And they'd end
up liking me. A teacher got me into a special
after-school art program. I started it, but I couldn't
continue because we moved again.

My aunt would always visit no matter where we
lived. She argued with my mom and dad. One day I
heard her say, "You're going to lose all of your
children." I got so scared, I felt sick. My sister Olivia
heard her say it also, and she started to cry. The
other children saw Olivia crying, and they cried, too.
I forced myself not to show that I was afraid, because
I had to quiet them down, but I cried inside. That's
where I still cry. But I made a promise to myself that
I would keep our family together.

I always found a store to work in, or some old
person to run errands for—things a kid could do. I
used to bag groceries at the supermarket so that I
could get tips. The store manager would give me
Cheerios, Kool-Aid, and milk to take home.
Sometimes we couldn't drink the milk because it was
spoiled.

My sisters and brothers depended on me. I had
to be there to take care of them. So you see, I didn't
have time to play like other kids. I was sorry, though,
that I couldn't take the special art class, but I still
drew every chance I got. I'd draw on any kind of

blank paper or napkin. One of the store clerks saw me drawing on the back of a match cover. A tiny drawing of a geranium. "Boy, you a genius," she said, and gave me a box of crayons.

I kept thinking that the bad times would only last a short while. My parents would get better and our life would be like before. That's what kept me being perfect in school and doing everything I could to help.

But everything kept getting worse no matter what I did, or how much I tried to help. First Ronald was taken away. My parents said it'd only be for a short time, until they got on their feet. We lived in one smelly room with all of us in it. No more paintings and music and flowers. The whole building was stinking. It was a shelter for homeless families. That was the last place we lived in and the last time my aunt visited us.

I almost stopped going to school then, because the first day I went, another kid pointed at me and said, "That's one of them homeless kids." But I was determined not to let them get to me. If I messed up, what would happen to the younger children?

I didn't feel homeless, not as long as we were all together. My parents watched over us and took good care of us. They weren't bad people, even though other people said that they were bad. They always told us, "We're sorry. We love you." Over and over

again. *"We're sorry. We love you. This isn't forever."*
They couldn't take care of us, but they worried about
us all of the time. The memories crowd my head.
This is not what you were writing to me about
anyway. I'll finish later.

Later,
12 midnight

Dear Doris,

I'm back. I had to stop writing you because I was
getting a terrible headache, but I want to finish telling
you my story. My dad died first, and it wasn't a car
accident. I made that up. He got so skinny and weak,
he looked like a living skeleton. My mother told me
that his health broke down and that he died of
pneumonia. Then Olivia was taken away one day
screaming and crying. My aunt and my mother
argued over the other children, but they stayed for a
time because I knew how to take care of them.

My mother used to tell us a story about when
she was a girl in her home in the South. One day she
was walking home from school with her friends.
She'd stopped to pick flowers for her mom, and a
goat started eating her notebook. All the kids tried to
chase the goat, but it would butt its head at them
and just continue chewing. We'd laugh so much.

She told the story every time we were having
problems and had to move, or my father was ill.

We'd add to the story to make it funnier. Olivia said that the goat ate the whole book and then started talking instead of bleating. One of the twins said the goat ate the book and started saying its abc's.

The last time my mother told the goat story, only I was with her, and she was in the hospital. She was so sick that she could hardly talk. She wanted to tell me the whole story, but I couldn't laugh. I started to cry inside when I saw that she was trying so hard to make me laugh.

The last thing she said to me was "You're my little prince, Amir. You're blessed. Don't lose your brothers and sisters."

After that the children were taken away, and I went to live with my aunt Gloria and her husband. But I didn't stay there very long. I started playing hookey from school, because now even the teachers looked at me strange. One day a kid asked me if I was dying of AIDS. Why would a kid say that to me? I was real skinny, but I wasn't sick. Maybe he'd heard a teacher say something about my family. Or maybe he'd heard rumors. A foster kid like me has official records and memories following him everywhere.

Doris, I could never say this to anyone but you. (I guess the social workers, counselors, caseworkers, etc. etc., know. I'm not even sure how much the Smiths know.) Both of my parents died of AIDS. They were drug addicts. Junkies. Druggies. Dope

Addicts. I can't believe I'm writing this about my own mother and father. Junkies and druggies. Maybe the more I write it, say it, the more words will just be words. Junkies, Druggies. Dope Addicts. Junkies. Druggies. Dope Addicts. Junkies. Druggies. Dope Addicts. I tell myself that these are words that don't matter.

I stopped going to school after my mom died and the children were put in foster care. I ran away from my aunt and went to live with my parents' friends in Brooklyn. I blamed my aunt for getting all of us kids separated. I blamed her for my parents' getting sick. I blamed her for everything. I wouldn't talk to her when she called me, and I ran wild in Brooklyn. I felt like some other person was inside of me. We never lived like that, even when my mom and dad were sick. I didn't draw anymore.

Then one night I dreamed that I saw my mother crying. That dream brought me back to my real self. I missed my brothers and sisters so much. How could I take care of them if I was all messed up?

Do you see why your letter about Charlene brought back bad memories? Do you understand, Doris? I hope you don't look down on me. My mom and dad weren't bad people. Sometimes I get angry about what happened, but I fight it because I don't want to hate the mother and father I love.

The Young Battle-Ax in the office said to me, "You are the most patient teenager with kids that I've

ever met. Where did you learn how to be so helpful?"
My mother and father taught me how. They were
good parents. That's what I want you to know and
believe.

Love,

Amir

P.S. I won the best counselor award. And I sent out
more letters last week. That takes care of all of the
names I had.

An owl hooted in the distance—a lonely sound.
Amir felt as if he could fly to wherever the owl was
and keep it company. Ronald snored lightly in the
next bed. It was a comforting sound. Amir put his
letter in an envelope. Maybe his memories were like
vampires; once they were exposed to Doris's light,
they'd be dead forever. Amir glanced at Ronald
again. His little brother was in a deep sleep. Amir
opened his sketchpad to a clean page. He began to
draw a picture of the lake and hoped Doris would
understand.

10 A.M.
Thursday
September 3rd

My Dear Amir,

I felt so bad when I read your letter this morning. How could you think I'd look down on you because of your parents? Our friendship is like steel, not glass. I'm sorry that my letter about Charlene made you think of such bad memories.

Your letter touched my heart so deep, I sat down and cried when I read it. You know I can cry easily. All I have to do is, like I always say, put myself in your sneakers, and that's what I did. I kept thinking, "Suppose it was me?" I know you were frightened by what happened to your family. I'd be.

I tried to think of some wonderful words I could say to make you feel better, but I can't. There are no words, only a feeling I have inside of me. All I can say is no matter what happens yesterday, today, or tomorrow, we're friends to the end.

Amir, I can't even picture how you tried to take care of everyone. Also, your letter proves to me that I was right all along: You are a hero. I couldn't have done what you did. Maybe I would've tried, but I would've fallen apart like an old dress. I would help my mom and dad and take care of them and Gerald if I could, but I don't know. Maybe I'd get mad sometimes, because it would be like I was the adult and they were the children. But

I'd love them and worry about them, because they'd still be my mother and father.

Amir, no matter how they got ill, they were ill, so that's all you have to say. If you introduced them to someone, you wouldn't say, "Hi, meet my junkies, my dope addicts, my crackheads." You'd say, "Meet my parents." That's all you ever have to say. My parents. Nothing can change that. I will never breathe a word of this to a living soul.

I have to make another point. I don't think it would matter to the Smiths what happened to your parents. They probably know anyhow. Like you said, the records follow you.

Please don't be sad.

Love,

Doris

Amir read Doris's letter a second and a third time. Her words were a gift. The unhappiness could settle back in that little corner of his brain and stay put.

He had just started to answer Doris's letter when the screen door downstairs banged loudly.

"Alvin? What's wrong? You'll break the door," Grace said, her voice raised enough for Amir to hear.

Alvin's voice was muffled, and Amir could make out only a word here and there. "Why? . . . After everything we did . . ."

He couldn't hear Grace's words at all, only the soft, murmuring sound of her voice.

"Amir!" Alvin shouted from the foot of the steps. He sounded as if he was standing in the bedroom with Amir. "Come down here this minute!"

Friends and Family

Amir was startled. He was accustomed to Alvin Smith bellowing, but it was usually with a loud laugh and a noisy "Big Papa's in the house." Taking two steps at a time, Amir rushed down the stairs to the kitchen.

Alvin held up a letter. "What's this all about?"

Amir flinched and backed away from him. Was he now seeing the other side of this man? Anger had twisted and distorted Alvin's face.

"Why did you do this?" Mr. Smith asked, thrusting a white envelope in Amir's face. "Why? Answer me."

"Do what, sir?" Amir asked. He held up his hands, protecting himself from the blows he thought Mr. Smith was getting ready to land on his face. Amir glanced for a moment at Grace Smith, his eyes frightened like a child's. She turned away.

"You sent a letter to a stranger. After I told you not to. How many of these have you sent out?" Alvin Smith's hands shook as he tore the letter out of the envelope and began to read it aloud.

"Dear Amir Smith,

"I just received your letter and would like to meet you so that we can discuss this matter. I know where your aunt and your brothers and sisters live. I would like to take you to them immediately. Write to me at the above P.O. number and give me your telephone number and/or e-mail address so that we can arrange a time and place to meet in Syracuse, NY, or anywhere you wish. Also, your artwork

is beautiful. I can help you sell some of your drawings too.

"Contact me as soon as you receive this letter.

"Sincerely,

"G. Jones"

Alvin threw the letter on the kitchen table. "He or she has the nerve to give an address. I'm contacting the police. I can't understand why you did this!"

"I wanted to find my brothers and sisters. I had to do something." Amir's lips trembled as he gazed at the letter. "Maybe this person is okay."

Grace stood between Amir and her husband. "Alvin, your pressure," she said.

"It was a dangerous, foolish thing to do." Alvin's voice rose, drowning out the sound of Ronald's basketball hitting the backboard in the yard. His angry breath overpowered the sweet smell of his wife's red-velvet cake.

"Calm down, Alvin. Amir meant no harm."

He turned to Grace. "Meant no harm? He disobeyed us. And was fixing to bring danger to himself."

Shame and anger warred in Amir's heart. *He had no right to open my mail. How did he find the letter?* Amir's head felt light. "But Mr. Alvin, maybe it's not a fake. Maybe the person knows something about them. . . ." He hesitated as tears welled up in his large eyes.

"It is a fake!" Alvin shouted.

Be determined. "But—but how do you know this

person's lying? The letter doesn't say anything bad." His father's voice ringing in his head strengthened him. He reached for the letter.

Mr. Smith snatched it off the table. "This is junk from a sick person who wants to molest a child!"

Amir looked on with disbelief as Alvin tore the letter into small pieces and threw them to the floor like confetti. Amir dropped to the floor and tried to put the tiny pieces together. "It was my letter. Why did you open my letter?"

Alvin shook the empty envelope in Amir's direction. "The mailman accidentally put the letter in the neighbor's mailbox. Bruce's mother handed it to me as I walked in. This nut wrote A. Smith on the envelope." He threw the envelope on the floor. "God is good. Made sure *I* got this letter. God takes care of children and fools, Amir. And you're both!"

"Alvin, please, that's enough." Grace clasped her husband's arm and shook him slightly. "We can finish this discussion at family devotions this evening."

He jerked his arm away from his wife. "I'm too angry for devotions. It ain't working no way."

Amir saw Alvin's face; it looked like rough brown tree bark. He saw his eyes drooping as he wiped them with the back of his hand. He heard his voice—low, scratchy, and drained of anger now.

"Why didn't you trust me, son? I told you I'd find them."

Finally, Amir was able to see Alvin Smith not only with his eyes but with his heart, and the tears rolled down his face, too. He tried to push them back, but he could no longer keep them inside. "I . . . I'm sorry, Pops. I didn't want to upset you. This person might know where they are."

Grace gasped slightly, and Alvin looked stunned.

"Don't push it, Alvin," Grace said firmly.

Amir sobbed as he still tried fruitlessly to piece the letter together.

Grace bent down on one knee, put her arm around Amir, and handed him a tissue. "This person is lying, Amir."

"But we . . . we could've checked."

Alvin's shoulders slumped. He slowly shook his head as he stood over Amir and Grace. "We don't need to check. Your aunt called me at work today. *That's* how I know this fool is lying."

Saturday morning
September 12th

Dear Doris,

When I received your letter last week I was so happy. First, I like the things you said about my mom and dad. Your words helped me. Maybe you have some words for Charlene. Maybe all she needs is a friend, Doris.

There has been so much excitement around here. That's why it took me so long to write you back. I have some unbelievable news. I spoke to my aunt Gloria last week! She was crying so much at first that we could hardly talk. She'd spent the last two years, she said, "Gathering up the little ones, taking them out of foster homes," and she and her husband adopted them. She tracked down Ronald, too, and was real happy to know that we lived together. She thought I was still living with a foster family in the Bronx. Seems like Mister Alvin and my aunt were tracking each other.

At first I thought that my aunt would yell and fuss like she used to do with my mother and father, but she just said that she was happy to hear my voice and know that Ronald and me were okay. She didn't even ask me why I wouldn't talk to her in the past, or why I ran away.

I wanted to say, "Auntie Gloria, I'm sorry for the way I acted," but I felt too shy, nervous, and embarrassed to say anything except "Hello, Auntie Gloria. How are the children?"

She is coming here today with her husband and all of my brothers and sisters. They'd been living in Virginia, but they just moved back to New York City and live in Brooklyn!

We have all been busy cleaning. Miss Grace's been cooking and baking, getting ready for their visit.

I've never seen her act so nervous. She even yelled at Ronald this morning!

My heart starts to beat fast when I think about seeing them all again. It'll be like a family reunion. Almost.

Before I go, I have to tell you about another strange and unbelievable event. Someone answered one of the letters I'd sent out, and Mister Alvin found it. The person was lying about knowing where my brothers and sisters were. Mister Alvin was so angry and upset, thinking I'd get snatched by a child molester or something, he almost cried.

He had the same look in his eyes my father had once when I'd been playing over at a friend's house for hours and he thought that I was lost. My father was angry and almost cried, too. For a minute I felt like Mister Alvin was my father for real, and I called him Pops. It just slipped out accidentally. I haven't said it again.

But I feel more like things are normal here since I said it. I know Mister Alvin would like to have a long discussion about why won't I keep calling him Pops. I don't know why myself. I apologized for sending out the letters, and he apologized for yelling at me. I'm going to paint a picture of Miss Grace and Mister Alvin. I haven't finished the picture of the lake yet, but I will. I always keep my promises.

Let me know what's happening in the Bronx.

Was there a Sunday school picnic this year? Did you go? Send me another issue of The Bronx News.

Gotta go now. My brothers and sisters will be here soon. Mister Alvin is calling me and Ronald. I hope this ain't a dream.

Love,

Amir

"Ronald, come on in here and get cleaned up."

"Aw, Papa, can I play one more game?"

"No. Come in now. Our company will be here soon."

Amir heard one last *bap* of the basketball before Ronald burst into the kitchen like a small explosion. "Can't I play until they get here?"

"No," Grace said. "You know we explained to you that your brothers and sisters are coming today, so you have to be on your best behavior and make them feel welcome."

"And they don't want to see a greasy little brother," Alvin joked. "Remember our talk last night? Remember we explained that when you were little, you came to live with us?"

Ronald nodded.

Grace rubbed his head. "Your mommy and daddy who brought you and Amir and your other brothers and sisters into this world are with God now."

Amir thought about Doris's explanation of the two kinds of family: *blood family and chosen family.* Ronald wouldn't understand that. Maybe nobody could understand it except him and Doris. So Amir said to Ronald, "Guardian angels. Our mother and father are guardian angels watching over us."

Grace and Alvin were both surprised that he'd added to the conversation.

"Yes," Alvin said, "Amir's right on with that. Guardian angels. That's a good thought, son."

Ronald nodded. "But you are my mama and papa now?"

"Yes," they both answered.

"What about Amir?"

"We're a special family, and Amir is part of it, too," Grace said.

"We're Amir's foster parents for now," Alvin quickly added.

"Will the other kids stay with us like Amir?" Ronald asked.

"They're visiting you and Amir," Alvin said.

"Do the boys play basketball or are they like you, Amir?"

Amir shrugged his shoulders. "Maybe they do, Ronald. I don't know, because I haven't seen them for a long time."

"Perhaps they're artists like Amir," Grace said, proudly holding the rough sketch of the portrait that Amir was planning to paint of her and Alvin.

"Or maybe they're good basketball players like you are," Alvin said.

Ronald spun around the kitchen as if he was dribbling a basketball. "I hope they're good artists like Amir. Then they all can draw pictures of me," he said, posing with the ball under his arm.

Amir smiled slowly as Ronald went back to dribbling the invisible basketball. Suddenly he felt connected to Ronald, just as he had when he first saw him in their mother's arms.

Alvin glanced out the window. "Here they come. They're rolling down the driveway now."

Before Alvin finished his sentence, Amir was out the door. Alvin's and Grace's mouths opened in shock. Even Ronald looked surprised to see Amir bursting with excitement, as though the two of them had traded places. Ronald watched Amir run down the driveway to meet the car, then suddenly followed him. As the car came to a stop, Ronald stood close to Amir. Amir put his arm around Ronald's shoulders while they waited for their sisters and brothers to climb out.

Grace and Alvin watched them sadly for a moment from the kitchen window before going outside to greet Amir's family.

10 P.M.

September 12th

Dear Doris,

I'm back again. I have to tell you about all of the things that happened today. I finally saw my sisters and brothers—and my aunt Gloria and her husband, Uncle Zachary. We always called him Uncle Z for short. It almost felt like a family reunion. At first everything was wonderful. My aunt almost jumped out of the car before it stopped—just like Ronald does when he's excited.

I remembered her—except she's shorter and fatter than my mom was, but their voices are the same. She squeezed me like a lemon and began to cry. The kids looked shocked. Ronald stood next to me with his mouth open and his eyes bugging out of his head. "Oh, my God, you look just like your father," my aunt said to me.

Her husband said, "You've grown so tall." (Maybe I'm as tall as you are now, Doris.) "And you finally got some meat on them bones." (He always said I was too skinny.)

Anyway, when Aunt Gloria turned toward Ronald, he looked like he wanted to run down the driveway and get away from her. I thought that she was going to smother him to death when she hugged him. My uncle kept saying to her, "Now, baby, calm down, baby." Ronald didn't seem to know whether to laugh or to cry.

The kids got out of the car, looking shy and confused, like they weren't sure what was happening. Ronald was shy, too, and seemed frightened—which was strange because he always loves to play with other kids. And here these other kids were his own sisters and brothers.

Of course, I remembered them all, though they have grown. Only my sister Olivia remembered me. She smiled, and I saw my mother's face again. Olivia hugged me. That's how she always was—smiling, hugging, happy. She hugged Ronald and even Miss Grace and Mister Alvin.

My aunt said, staring at the younger ones, "I always told them that they had two brothers, and they were crazy with excitement all the way up here. Now see how they're acting."

We all went in the house, and Ronald and the other kids just stared at each other, I guess the same way me and Ronald looked at each other when we first met. I whispered to Ronald, "Ask them whether they want to play ball."

"You play basketball?" he asked Shawn and David.

They lit up like little lamps. "Yeah, yeah." All four of them, including Sharon, the other twin, dashed out of the house. Olivia and I followed them. Olivia grabbed my hand as we walked toward the bench, and it felt like we'd never been separated.

We sat on the bench together and watched the others play ball. Sharon played as good as the boys. Olivia whispered to me, "She's a wild tomboy, you know."

After a while I got my sketchpad, and with Olivia sitting next to me on the bench, I drew her. She has a smile like my mother's—the same deep dimples. Then I sketched Ronald, David, and the twins playing ball. I wish I could sketch the sound of their laughter, and I wish I could sketch the happiness in my heart. I wasn't thinking about anything. Not about what happened in the past, or even what would happen in the future.

Mister Alvin grilled hamburgers and franks, and Miss Grace brought out potato salad, fried chicken, and one of her layer cakes, and we all stuffed ourselves. Uncle Z and Mister Alvin watched a baseball game on television. My aunt helped Miss Grace serve the food.

Everything was beautiful until my aunt and uncle took me aside so that they could speak to me privately. I sat between both of them on the porch swing, and my aunt spoke first. "This is a nice place, Amir, and the Smiths are good people," she said. "But they're not your real family."

Then my uncle said, "Your aunt wants all of you kids to live together. You don't know how worried she's been about you."

Aunt Gloria held my hand like she didn't want me

to get away. "Amir, we want you and Ronald to live with us. That's what your mother wanted, too."

"Ronald thinks the Smiths are his family," I said.

"I know, but see how happy he is with his sisters and brothers—and with you. This is what your mother worried about more than anything—that you kids would end up living in different homes. I know, because she told me."

She clutched my hand until it hurt. "It's only left now for you and Ronald to be with us."

Uncle Zachary said, "It won't be easy, because we have two teenagers of our own. Your cousins. They're anxious to see you."

"Me and your uncle are working hard to keep things going as it is." Aunt Gloria looked real worried. "But you and Ronald are family—my sister's children. You don't know how it upset me that you were in a group home somewhere and Ronald didn't even know his own family."

She held my face in both of her hands like I was a little kid. "I've prayed many times for this day. Amir, since you're fourteen, it's up to you to say where you want to live. You can stay here, but you know what your dear mother would've wished."

My uncle jumped into the conversation. "There might be a little fight when it comes to Ronald, because the Smiths want to adopt him," he said, "and I don't think they'll give up so easy. But Ronald will get used to living with us." Uncle Zachary kept wiping his sweaty forehead with a handkerchief, like he was nervous.

My aunt and uncle told me that there would be a hearing before a judge, and I'd have to speak with a social worker. "You're important to all of this, Amir," she said. "If you say you want to live with us and you want all of your sisters and brothers to be together, then the judge will most likely agree to let all you children live with me and your uncle."

All sorts of feelings swept over me, Doris. I could hear the kids playing in the backyard—laughing, screeching, with Olivia watching and calling them, because she's the big sister. They made a lot of happy noise—the way you always want your family to sound. But all I could think about was how those happy sounds would change soon.

First, I felt sorry for Miss Grace and Mister Alvin. Second, I felt bad for Ronald. I couldn't imagine him living anywhere but here. What made me feel real bad was that my aunt was right. My mother and father had wanted all of us to live together.

Well, when it was time for them to leave, Ronald wanted to know whether they were coming back tomorrow. Then the kids started jumping up and down yelling, "Can we come back tomorrow? Can we?"

My aunt didn't answer them. "It's getting late now. We have to go" was all she said.

And my uncle said, "You all had a good time today. You'll see your brothers again."

I hated to see them go, too, but I couldn't bear to look at Miss Grace and Mister Alvin.

My aunt and uncle must've told them they wanted to adopt Ronald, because both of them seemed so sad. After everyone had gone, Miss Grace went to her bedroom, and Mister Alvin took me and Ronald out for a ride. I know he wanted to talk to us, but he was silent, which is not like him. Ronald didn't know anything yet, so he just chattered on and on about the visit. He's sleeping in the other twin bed now, probably having happy dreams.

When we got back from the ride, the whole house felt different. Now I hear Miss Grace's and Mister Alvin's voices coming from downstairs. I can't tell what they're saying—just soft voices sounding like a moan. I'm trying not to be angry with my aunt, because she's following my mother's wishes. But this reminds me of the way she used to upset my mother whenever she visited us. I tell myself that she's only trying to help.

I always thought that all of us being together would make life perfect. And it was for a little while this afternoon. But now I'm more confused than before. I hated to see everyone leave, and part of me wanted to go with them. But I didn't want to hurt the Smiths, and I know I'd miss Ronald, too. It's just like you said once before. Someone is going to end up unhappy.

Love,

Amir

Amir was worn out. He put the letter in the same envelope with the letter he'd written earlier that day. He wanted to go to sleep like Ronald and not think about things anymore.

He heard a soft knock on the door before Alvin opened it. "Come downstairs for a moment, son. We have to talk to you," Alvin whispered. Ronald stirred in his sleep.

Amir felt as though someone had placed a pile of rocks on his slender shoulders as he followed Alvin to the living room.

Grace's gentle brown eyes were rimmed in red. Though she put on her glasses when Amir sat next to her on the couch, he could tell she'd been crying.

Alvin cleared his throat. "Amir, this is hard. Your aunt and uncle told us that you'll be going to live with them."

Amir stared directly at Alvin and shook his head. "I didn't tell her anything yet. I mean . . . I guess I will."

Grace tried to steady her voice. "We . . . we understand if you want to go with your aunt. We would love for you to stay with us and would adopt you, adopt—"

Alvin finished for her. "We would adopt you also, Amir. The choice is yours." He cleared his throat. "But Ronald has to stay with us. Because your aunt requested a hearing about his case, we can't go on with the adoption proceedings." He leaned back in his chair and rubbed his forehead as if he had a headache. "We want you to know that we will fight to keep Ronald. We are not trying to split up your family, but we raised Ronald since he was a toddler." He paused and stared at Amir. "Do you understand, son?"

Amir nodded and lowered his eyes. "Yes," he barely whispered. The weight felt heavier—he just wanted to go to sleep. *Buck up, you guys.* His father's words didn't help this time.

"Amir, Ronald is our son. He could see his brothers and sisters often. Call them every day if he wants to. But we can't just give him up like that. What would it do to him?"

Ronald suddenly burst into the room. "I don't want to go away," he cried. "Please don't send me away. Please, Papa!" He jumped into Grace's lap, and she rocked him.

Alvin said, "Come on, Ronald, you too big for all that. Nobody's going to send you away." His voice cracked. He rubbed his mustache and tried to make a joke. "Every shut eye ain't asleep."

Ronald slid off Grace's lap and sat between her and Amir. His button eyes filled with tears as he turned to Amir and grabbed his arm. "I don't want you to leave. I want you to stay here, too."

Amir's throat tightened. He couldn't speak, but he put his arm around Ronald's shoulders.

4 P.M.
Thursday
September 17th

My Dear Amir,

I thought you'd be jumping up and down for joy about finally being with all your sisters and brothers. I know what I said before about someone getting hurt. But why does it always have to be like that? There's got to be a way to fix things and make them perfect for everyone involved.

Now, I reread one of your letters, and you said that your mother told you not to lose your brothers and sisters. Well, you haven't lost them, because you know where they are. She didn't say everyone had to live together, did she?

Anyway, I felt so bad for you when I read your letter. Ronald will be tripping if they take him away from the Smiths. Your aunt and uncle put you in the middle of everything. Well, here are some words that I hope will help you.

People do not have to live in the same house, or on the same street, in the same state, or in the same country in order to be close to one another. Sometimes people see each other every day and can't stand one another anyhow.

It doesn't matter who lives where or who lives with who. Everyone can't be in the same place all at once. But hearts can remember and love all of the time.

Amir, I hope by now you have decided what you are going to do. I know you didn't ask for my advice or my opinion, but I've been thinking about your situation and here's a little tip:

Go with your aunt and uncle. It makes sense. Suppose the court sends Ronald to live there. The best place for him to be is wherever *you* are, because you are Ronald's memory. You understand his old life with the Smiths, and you can help him with his new life with his real family. Ronald is old enough to write letters. He can write the Smiths and that way never lose touch with them. He might be upset at first, but he'll get used to it. I hope this is helpful.

I didn't create a new issue of The Bronx News yet, because, like I said, I'm only telling good news. For a time last week there was nothing good to report; as a matter of fact, it was turning into the worst week of my life.

As you know, at first when I found out about Charlene, I decided to end our friendship. Let her run wild with her sisters or whoever. She stopped meeting me in the library and coming around the block after she told me what she was doing. I decided not to say anything to anybody, because I'm no snitch.

On Monday Gerald made a serious effort to drive me crazy, so I took him to the library. You will not believe who was already there—all of Charlene's sisters. They couldn't find Charlene and thought that she was with me. "You got our sister all messed up," one of the older sisters says. "Trying to be a cool little twerp like you," says she.

"How come you don't know where your own sister is?" says I.

"Don't get smart with me," says she, and so on. You get my drift. Then another sister says, "She ain't been acting right since y'all become buddies."

I felt like I was hit with a bolt of lightning. They really didn't know what Charlene was doing. She wasn't following behind them but doing her own stupid thing.

So, Amir, I took your advice. I found some words to help Charlene. I told. I could barely say it out loud. "Your sister's been smoking pot." I felt rotten, and all I could hear was Charlene's sisters screeching in my ears like 100 sirens tearing down Third Avenue.

"You a liar."

"You the one been spreading those rumors."

"We told Charlene she was stupid to be friends with you."

"You no different from them other girls."

"Why don't you listen? Your sister needs help," I said.

The oldest sister shut the other ones up. "Charlene been acting strange. Sometimes she'd be like the sister she was supposed to be, and other times she'd act like she wanted no part of us around her."

"You going to tell your mother?" I asked.

"Have to."

"What will she do?"

"Kill her."

Amir, you can imagine how I felt, but things got even worse, and I began to wish that I'd minded my own business. Charlene and I had promised to keep each other's secrets. Now hers were all over the Bronx because of me. The rumor factory got to working overtime. People said that I caused Charlene to be sent to a home for juvenile delinquents.

Even my mother heard. Nosy Nichols told her that I'd gotten Charlene in trouble. I told her the whole story even though I didn't want to. I was afraid I'd be under punishment until I was fifty years old if I didn't.

My mother surprised me, though. She didn't rant and rave. All she asked was "You didn't try it, did you?"

"No."

"Don't lie to me. Kids try things. But I don't want you to lie to me about it."

"Ma, the truth, the God's honest truth, I didn't." My mother always knows when I'm lying anyhow. Says she can see the word *LIAR* flashing in each eyeball like a neon sign when I'm not telling the truth. So she let up. But she wouldn't let go. She decided to talk to Charlene's mother herself.

I begged her not to. "You don't even know her that well."

"I'll get to know her now. If it was you, Doris, I'd want her to tell me. We have to protect all of you kids. I'm talking to Charlene's mother in case those sisters forget to tell her what's going on."

I understand what the word "humiliated" means now. So much more than embarrassed. I was mortified, humiliated, ashamed. No one spoke to me—only Yellow Bird, who told me that people were saying that I was a snitch and that my mother was a busybody.

I learned a new word: *PARIAH*

Last year my teacher tried to teach us that word, but it wasn't interesting to me, so I ignored her. But now I know the word. It's me. Here's an old corny joke: From now on, when they define the word "pariah" in the dictionary, my picture will be next to it. Outcast, outsider, hated person. Everyone is angry with me— even Lavinia and the twins, who don't like Charlene.

And to top it all off, my father was looking in the phone book for the number of some man in Manhattan and found that a page was torn out. He's been mumbling and grousing about it ever since.

Well, Amir, I'm going to end this letter. My mother is taking me to the store to buy some extra school supplies. School started last week. But this is not the end of my story. Some surprising things happened at the Sunday school picnic. Will tell you all about it the next time I write.

I hope you are not feeling too sad and that everything will turn out perfect for you and your family.

Gotta go now.

Love,

Doris

part five

Lost and Found

Amir folded Doris's letter neatly and put it back in his jacket pocket. He'd read it for the second time. Her words echoed in his head, and whether she knew it or not, they were helping him decide what to do. It was strange, he thought, that he'd received her letter the very morning he and Ronald and the Smiths had left the house to come here to the family court hearing.

All during the car ride he'd thought about what he'd say. He'd tried to block out Ronald's incessant questions: "Will the judge put me in jail?" "Will he send me away?" "Is Amir talking to the judge, too?" "When will my brothers and sisters be back?" "Are they talking to the judge?" "Will they be there?"

Grace and Alvin had reassured Ronald. "Don't worry." "Everything is okay." "You're not going to jail, silly."

Now he and Amir were sitting in the family court waiting room. Amir glanced at the large oak doors leading to the judge's chambers. He wondered what was going on. Was Uncle Zachary nervously wiping his sweaty forehead? Was Aunt Gloria angry? Was Miss Grace crying and Mister Alvin demanding something?

Ronald had already made a friend. He and another boy his age were looking through a sports magazine for kids. Amir wished he had his sketchpad so he could draw the other children and people sitting around the waiting room.

The door to the judge's chambers opened, and his aunt and uncle and the Smiths walked out. All their faces looked like stone. Amir could hardly bear to meet their gaze. For a moment he would have liked to crawl under one of the coffee tables in the room and hide. He thought about his parents. Why did you guys leave me in all this confusion?

The guard motioned for Amir to enter the judge's chambers. As he crossed the room, his aunt stared at him, making him feel guilty. "Think about your dear mother and what she wanted," she said sharply.

Grace looked as if she'd been crying, but he wasn't sure. It seemed as though she was always crying since his aunt's visit.

Mister Alvin cut his eyes at Aunt Gloria and then smiled at Amir. "It's going to be all right, son. Whatever you decide is okay."

Grace nodded. "We'll be fine. We're all still on the same planet." She tried to smile.

Amir entered a large room with books lining the wall. The guard motioned for him to sit before the judge, who was looking over some papers. Amir's heart beat fast, and his hands felt clammy. He tried to calm himself by remembering what his father used to tell him: *When you help someone else, you help yourself, too.* He remembered Doris's words as well: *You are Ronald's memory.*

The judge finally looked up and smiled at Amir. "How are you? Amir? Amir Daniels?"

"Yes, ma'am, that's right. I'm fine." He calmed down a little because something about the judge's round face and smooth tan complexion reminded him of Miss Grace.

"I'm Judge Michaels. Do you know why you're here?"

"Yes, ma'am."

"Relax now. I'm not going to hurt you. We just want to do what's best for you and your brothers and sisters. Have you been happy and comfortable living with the Smiths?"

"Yes. They're very nice foster parents."

"I see here you lived with your aunt for a short time, and then you moved?"

"Yes."

"Were you happy with your aunt?"

"I was upset about my parents."

"So you didn't leave because of your aunt and uncle?"

"No, ma'am. They took good care of me."

"I understand. What about your brother Ronald. You and he getting along?"

"Yes."

"Do you think he's happy living with the Smiths?"

"He loves them. He thinks they're his parents."

The judge paused and gave Amir a long look. "What do you want to do? Your aunt is requesting that you and Ronald live with her and the other children. She and your uncle are prepared to care for all of you. Now, tell me: Where do you want to live?"

Amir licked his dry lips. "Wherever Ronald lives."

The judge looked at him over her glasses. "You mean that you don't want to live with the Smiths?"

"I like living with them. They're real good parents."

"I'm trying to understand, you don't want to live with your aunt?"

"I want to live with Ronald. Wherever he has to live."

"Son, you're not really telling me anything. Your aunt wants you, and the court prefers to keep children in a family together if at all possible. So I wish you'd give me an answer."

"I'm Ronald's memory, ma'am, so I have to stay with him. Wherever he goes, I'll go along with him."

"You don't care where you live?"

"I do care, but I'm used to living in different places. But Ronald only knows about living with the Smiths."

"Are you saying that Ronald shouldn't go with your aunt so that all of you children can be together? Do you think that he should stay with the Smiths?"

"Yes."

"So you want to live with the Smiths, too?"

Amir hesitated, but only for a moment. "Yes, ma'am."

Wednesday evening
September 23rd

Dear Doris,

Please don't feel like you did the wrong thing by helping Charlene. I think it's good you told her sisters. Don't worry about what people say. You know the truth, and you didn't get her in trouble—you probably kept her out of bigger trouble. Maybe her mother is making her stay in the house and that's why you don't see her. People tell lies. I don't think she's in a home for bad kids. You did the right thing.

Things have not been so great around here either. I mean Miss Grace and Mister Alvin are still kind to me—that never changes no matter what, but everything feels sad.

Mister Alvin isn't noisy and cracking jokes, and Miss Grace isn't baking as much as she used to—only when she has to for a customer. We didn't go to the lake or barbecue for Labor Day because it rained.

Even Ronald is tripping. Whining all the time and complaining that he doesn't want to go to school. A third-grade dropout. Maybe he's afraid that he'll come home from school and everyone will be gone. He told me he wants me to stay with him. Can you believe that?

We had the hearing today and I spoke to the judge. Even though I didn't follow your advice, your letter helped me more than you know. I was feeling like I was split in two. All I could do was think about this situation until it made me crazy—going backward and forward in my mind. But your words and Ronald begging me to stay helped me to make a decision.

I told the judge I wanted to stay with Miss Grace and Mister Alvin, because I felt that if I said I wanted to go with my aunt and uncle, then the judge would make Ronald go with them, too. Now we're waiting to hear what the judge decides.

I haven't told this to anyone else yet. Doris, I want to make everyone happy, but I can't. There's no perfect solution. Mostly, I worry about Ronald and the Smiths. I'm used to being sad, but Ronald isn't. I'm seeing that Mister Alvin and Miss Grace really are his mom and dad. If the judge sends Ronald with my aunt, then I'll ask to go with him. On the other hand, though, if he goes with my aunt, we'll be living in the city again! All of us together. Brooklyn is not perfect, but it's closer to the Bronx than Syracuse is. But I'd still feel sorry for Mister Alvin and Miss Grace.

School started up here, too, but I haven't been

thinking about school or anything else. I'll let you know what happens.

Doris, I haven't forgotten about the drawing of the lake. Trust me, you'll get it.

Love,

Amir

THE BRONX NEWS
Final Issue
Editor, Star Reporter, and Owner,
DORIS WILLIAMS

Monday, September 28th
TODAY'S WEATHER: Perfect—warm with a touch of fall crispness

NEWS FEATURE: The Labor Day/
Sunday School Picnic
by D. Williams

The Sunday school picnic is another major event of the year on 163rd Street. This one was no different. It seemed like everyone who'd been at the block party was also at the picnic—including Charlene's sisters and their mother; only Charlene was missing. The picnic was held at Bear Mountain.

Charlene's sisters, Doris, and her ex-friends rode

the same bus. All of the parents were on it, too. Since there is so much bad feeling among the kids, instead of piling up in the back of the bus so that they could play around and have fun, all of them sat near the front with the adults.

Only Charlene's sisters sat in the back of the bus, and they were quiet, which was very scary.

The adults laughed and told corny jokes—even Miss Connie, Charlene's mother. Would Miss Connie be this happy if her daughter was in some kind of juvenile home? Doris wondered. And would she be laughing and joking with Doris's mom if she thought that she was a busybody?

When they reached Bear Mountain, they found a good spot near the basketball and volleyball courts, with plenty of tables to put the food out on and trees to spread the blankets under. As soon as they had everything laid out, the Sunday school picnic began. Russell, Yellow Bird, and the other boys were everywhere—trying to get as much food as they could from their own mothers and everyone else's.

Doris had a sad conversation with her mother.

Mother: Doris, what's wrong?

Doris: Nothing.

Mother: I think there is. Seems to me you don't bother with your friends anymore.

Doris: Everyone hates me. They call me a snitch.

Her mother put her arm around her. "Doris, it's not

always easy to do what's correct. But I don't want you
to ever feel bad about doing what's right! Me and your
daddy are proud of you. Because you told about
Charlene, the block association is getting even more
serious about cleaning up that playground."

Her mother's words did not make Doris feel any
better about telling on Charlene.

So Doris looked at the trees with their fat dark
green leaves and the clear blue sky. There wasn't a
cloud anywhere except the one that hung over her
shoulder. Doris tried very hard not to feel lonely as
she watched everyone else running, playing,
laughing, and talking. Then the games began.

First there was the usual potato-sack race, which
Yellow Bird and Big Russell won. The volleyball game,
boys against girls, put Charlene's sisters, Lavinia, and
the twins on the same team. When one of the twins
made a good serve, one of the sisters yelled, "Go,
twin." Then they gave each other high fives when the
boys missed their serve. Perhaps they'd forgotten that
they didn't like each other.

Then the most unexpected event occurred. Doris
felt a tap on her shoulder. It was Miss Connie,
Charlene's mama. "Hi, baby," she said. "Can I talk to
you for a moment?"

Doris nodded and had trouble looking Charlene's
mother in the face. She thought the woman was
going to bless her out for talking about her daughter.

Instead Miss Connie said, "I just wanted to thank you, sweetie, for telling us about Charlene. She's with her grandparents down South and is doing well. And as for that wild T.T., he just got put out of gangster academy. I talked to his father, and Mr. T.T. is in serious trouble."

The cloud hanging over Doris's shoulder began to vanish. Maybe she wasn't a pariah anymore.

The girls won the volleyball game, and everyone got ready for the father-son basketball game, scrambling to get the best place to sit and watch the men lose to the boys like they do every year. Doris made a momentous decision. She owed Lavinia and the twins an apology, but they owed her one, too.

He ex-friends were sitting at one of the picnic tables, and as Doris walked over to them, she wasn't sure what she was going to say or how she was going to say it.

The twins ignored her, but Lavinia, whose mouth is never still, said, "Well, look who's here."

"I'm apologizing for calling you liars," Doris said very quickly, before she changed her mind.

Lavinia crossed her arms in front of her chest. "You want to be friends again, huh?"

"I just wanted to apologize, that's all. But you owe me an apology, too."

"For what?" one of the twins asked.

"Because you weren't completely correct. The sisters weren't fooling with drugs"

"Yeah, only your buddy Charlene."

"And that's not all true, either," Doris said.

Lavinia held up her hand like she was some kind of spokeswoman for the group.

"We apologize, too, for all of the things we said about you, but you can't be on the team again. We have a replacement for you."

"I don't want to be on the team," Doris said.

Lavinia made a space for Doris on the bench, and they nearly died laughing as they watched the boys wear the men out on the basketball court. It was a beautiful day.

ADVERTISEMENT

Still waiting for one drawing of a lake

OBITUARY

Yellow Bird and his family are moving!

Big Russell and his family are moving, too!

My Dear Amir,

So now you have the end of the story. I guess you could say the Sunday school picnic was a success, and I am no longer the most hated girl in the Bronx. But I'm glad this crazy summer is over.

Middle school is so different. Instead of having one annoying and boring teacher throughout the day, now I have five—one for every subject. (Just joking. The teachers are okay.)

I feel better because of what Charlene's mother said, but I don't feel totally good. Charlene is like a little itch on the back of my head that I can't scratch. She probably still thinks that I'm the worst person in the world. By the way, I heard that T.T. is handcuffed to his daddy and can't go nowhere without him.

Have you heard yet from the family court? What did the judge have to say? Will you be moving back to the city? We will always be friends to the end no matter where we live.

Love,

Doris

Friday evening
October 9th

Dear Doris,

I'm glad to see that The Bronx News is back. But no more issues? You're not the worst person in the world. I think you need to stop feeling bad about Charlene. One day she'll understand.

I am sorry I took so long to write you back, but I wanted to wait until I had some real news to tell you.

It's been so hard waiting every day to hear what the judge's decision would be. Mister Alvin said that no matter what she said, he'd continue the fight. "Take it all the way to the United States Supreme Court."

Mister Alvin tried to joke, but he wasn't like his old self. He never once asked me what I'd said to the judge. The old Mister Alvin would've been pumping me for information until Miss Grace made him give it up. He wanted to stop having family devotions, too, but Miss Grace insisted. The same thing was bothering all of us, so there was no reason to talk about that. Miss Grace would just read a short Bible verse and call it a night. It was too hard for them to do more than that, because they didn't know how long we'd be a family.

Yesterday I heard Miss Grace say, "His blood relatives have rights, too. Maybe we need to think about the reality. After all, we're just foster parents." And then she began to cry. But she always kept her usual smile for Ronald. He's in school, and trying to play basketball and look at all of the television he can get away with looking at.

In the meantime I finished the Smiths' portrait for them. I was just trying to make them feel a little better, but I realized while we were waiting that I really want to be here. Being here doesn't mean I'll be separated from the rest of my family, now that I know where they are.

Well, Doris, yesterday we finally heard from the judge and found out what her decision was. The judge said that Ronald was in a good home that he was accustomed to. She said that I could remain with Ronald also, since that's what I said I wanted to do. She also said that Ronald and I would have regular visits with our other siblings. But the Smiths have full custody of Ronald, and his adoption proceedings can continue.

Mister Alvin asked me whether I really wanted to stay here, and I said, "Yes, Pops." The words slipped out of my mouth so easy, not accidentally like before. "Now I can't picture myself living anywhere else."

Mom Smith cried when I said that. She's like you, Doris, She even cries over television shows.

I called my aunt and told her what I'd done. Well, she wasn't too happy, as you can imagine. She said that she thought I was being pressured. "My home is as good as anyone else's," she said. "We're your family. Your brothers and sisters are still worrying me and your uncle about going back up there. What were you thinking?"

She was so upset, I couldn't even talk to her. That's my aunt. "Auntie Gloria, I'm sorry for the way I treated you after my mother died, and for running away from you," I said. "And I promise to always stay close to all of you."

She was still upset when she put down the telephone. Pops said that she'll get over it.

The kids got on the phone then to talk to me and Ronald. You should've heard them. "Can we visit you again? When you coming to see us? Can you and Ronald come here tomorrow?" They sounded like they were fighting each other for the phone.

Mom and Pops say there's no reason why we can't spend holidays and vacations together, and they say that me and Ronald can call them as often as we want to. When I am grown, I can help take care of them, too.

High school isn't bad. The seniors look like grown men and women, and I see some ruffians roaming around, but I just stay out of their way. I'm in an honors art class, which I really like. We have to do a project, and I'm going to create a family album—blood family and chosen family—for my sisters and brothers. I'm sort of like an album myself, because like you once said, I hold all the memories— the good ones and the bad. Yesterday Mom Smith said something very nice to me. "As long as you think about your parents, they are never gone. They will always live in your heart."

I was so touched all I could do was nod my head. But one day I will tell her that my mother and father have always lived inside of me. The only difference is that now they have moved over and made space for her and Pop Smith.

Love,

Amir

P.S. I hope you like this drawing of yourself swimming in the lake. Did I make your arms long enough?

9 A.M.
Saturday
October 17th

My Dear Amir,

I love the drawing. I showed it to my mother and she says that you are unusually talented. I feel like I'm really there swimming in the lake in all of that cool blue water.

I hope that everything is fine up there in Syracuse. I think you made a good decision. To tell you the truth, I'm glad you're staying with Ronald at Mom and Pop Smith's. They are too nice to hurt. About those high school thugs—just do what you do best. Draw pictures of them and chill them out.

So much has happened since I last wrote to you. I've joined the student newspaper staff. I also joined

the track team. And you know what? I love it!
Imagine that! I'm not too bad, either. The coach says
that I have running legs—long and lean. Guess
what—my teammates call me Bean. That's my new
nickname, short for Stringbean (smile). When I run
they yell, "There goes Bean, the running machine."

I don't see Lavinia and the twins much because
we're all in different homeroom classes. I see one of
Charlene's sisters sometimes in the hall at school.
Yesterday, I got the best surprise. She handed me a
note from Charlene. Here is some of what Charlene
said.

*I guess you're surprised to hear from me—the
friend you betrayed. I hated you. I thought that my
sisters were right about you—that you were just like
all of the others.*

*Needless to say, I don't hate you anymore. Now
I'm glad you told because I'm happy here with my
grandparents in South Carolina. They are spoiling me
big time. It's just me and them. They let me read to
my heart's content—after chores. But I miss my
dopey sisters sometimes and I miss my mother. I miss
our trips to the library, too.*

*I like my school. The kids are not that different
from kids in the Bronx. A whole lot of them are doing
the same things. Someone's mama got busted for
growing marijuana in their backyard. That's worse
than the Bronx.*

I promised everyone—my grandparents, my mother, and my sisters, and most of all myself—that I will never mess with anything again. I don't know why I did it. Maybe I just went a little crazy. Hope we're still friends.

Charlene gave me her address, so that I can write her and give her all of the Bronx news. I might have to start up the newspaper again since all of my best friends are living someplace else. And soon I will be, too.

I guess the real big news, Amir, is that we will be moving from 163rd Street. My parents just told me. They're buying a small house (my mother says it's so tiny, it looks like a dollhouse, but it will be ours) on Long Island near my aunt. You know, Amir, I can't imagine living anywhere else except on 163rd Street. I guess the thought of leaving makes me sad and happy at the same time—a little like you used to be. I'll have my own room, instead of a space that we make believe is a room. Anyway, it won't be for a few months.

It doesn't matter, though, where we live—you and I. You'll always be my one true friend. I have to go now. The track team is practicing this morning.

Write soon.

Love,

Doris (Bean)